DEFIANT QUEEN

BOOK TWO OF THE MOUNT TRILOGY

MEGHAN

MARCH

Editor: Pam Berehulke
Bulletproof Editing
www.bulletproofediting.com

Cover design: @ Letitia Hassar
RBA Designs
www.RBADesigns.com

Cover photo: @ Sara Eirew
www.saraeirew.com

Interior Formatting: Champagne Book Design

Visit my website at www.meghanmarch.com.

DEFIANT QUEEN

ABOUT THIS BOOK

I'm his entertainment. His toy. Payment on a debt.

I tell myself I hate him, but every time he walks into the room, my body betrays me. How can I want him and fear him in the same moment?

They told me he'd mess with my head. Make it go to war with my body.

But I didn't realize it would be complete anarchy.

I should've known better. When Mount's involved, there are no rules.

I will not surrender. I will not show weakness. I'll stand my ground and make it out of this bargain with my heart and soul intact.

But he has other plans . . .

Defiant Queen is the second book in the Mount Trilogy.

ONE

Mount

Thirty years earlier

A DARK, CREEPY FEELING, LIKE I'D WALKED OVER someone's grave, slithered down my spine as the girl climbed the broken front steps of the porch with the social worker. The thin blonde clutched a black trash bag to her chest as they came through the ripped screen door. I didn't have to be a genius to guess that everything she owned was inside.

Me and my trash bag had moved fourteen times in the last nine years. I couldn't remember how many times I was passed around before that. My first memory was my stomach gnawing on itself, so I'd begged for more dinner and my foster dad had backhanded me across the face. I was four, or so they told me. It was hard to keep track when you never saw candles on a birthday cake because you ain't never had one.

I'd bet if Mrs. Holiday was still alive, I would've got

one, maybe even every year, but she got real sick and they moved me to a new house after six months when it was clear she wasn't gonna make it long and couldn't take care of us. First time I'd ever felt like someone wanted me. First time someone let me pick out my own clothes at a store. First time someone asked what I wanted for dinner. First time I ever felt like I had a real mom. All that did was make it harder when she was gone. It taught me to never get attached to anything or anyone in this life because there was nothing good down that road.

Every house before and after hers were different versions of the same old shit. You weren't one of their *real* kids; you were the paycheck they didn't do nothing to earn. Barely fed you. Lucky if you got a toothbrush from some of them. And clothes? Whatever the church donated or maybe what the real kids grew out of. Nothing new, that was for damn sure.

The undershirt I was wearing right now was more stained than white, and when I caught it on a chain-link fence earlier this week and ripped a hole in it, Jerry shoved me up against the side of the house and whipped off his belt to teach me a lesson, something he liked to do a few times a week, especially after he'd finished a six-pack and had a few smokes.

Mean drunks weren't nothing new either. I could spot them at a hundred yards now.

If Jerry didn't have a foot and a hundred fifty pounds on me, I would've hit him back the first time he pulled that belt free. Well, that, and knowing that if I got kicked out of this house, there was no one to protect Destiny. She was only six, but I saw the way Jerry looked at her. It wasn't right, so I did my best to stick as close to her as I could.

More times than not, I sneaked out of my room at night and slept in front of her door, just to make sure he didn't try nothing. I didn't trust that piece of shit as far as I could throw him, and with that fat fuck, it wasn't far.

"We're so excited to be able to place Destiny and her sister together, finally. Everyone, say hi to Hope," the social worker said, as much hope in her voice as the girl's name. She didn't get that there was no hope in this house, even with her here.

No hope in the whole fucked-up system.

Destiny's short, skinny legs flew across the room as she threw herself at the girl's waist while Jerry and his wife, Dixie, and their son, Jerry Jr., watched from a few feet away. He didn't get real close anymore. Probably because Jerry and Dixie only let me shower once a week. Saving on the water bill, or so they said.

When the new girl dropped the trash bag to hug her little sister, Jerry ran his tongue over his teeth, eyeing her like she was one of those thick steaks he brought home from the butcher to cook only for himself.

Lead settled in my gut when I realized she was older than I thought, despite being so small. Probably older than me. She already had tits, and definitely wasn't wearing a bra.

Jerry couldn't take his eyes off those tits of hers, and he wasn't even trying to hide it.

If the way he looked at Destiny wasn't right, the

way he looked at Hope was downright fucked up. I'd found his porno mags stuffed into a box in the lean-to where he thought no one would see them. He liked them young and blond, and I wanted to yell at the social worker to take both girls and get them as far away from this house as possible.

But I knew what'd happen if I shot my mouth off. I'd be the one who got booted, and there wouldn't be no one to protect either of them from Jerry.

"Missed you so much," Hope whispered to Destiny as she dropped to her knees on the dirty linoleum floor. They hugged long and hard before Hope looked up to take in the rest of us.

Jerry stepped forward first, of course. His gut strained against his white tank top as he held out his arms. "I'm your new daddy, Hope. Welcome home."

Hope's eyes widened, and she looked behind him until she caught sight of me. Like recognized like. She knew I wasn't one of the *real* kids. I shook my head just an inch to give her the warning.

I had to give the girl credit—she was quick on picking up signals, which blew, because that meant she'd been through shit that would make me go ballistic.

She kept Destiny hugged to her side and did one of those side-pat things with Jerry, but that bastard was persistent. He squeezed both girls in a hug.

"Feels like our little family's complete now."

Dixie gave her a nod. She didn't say much, probably because she spent as much of the day as possible drinking from a Sprite two-liter bottle. Except there were no bubbles in it, and when she passed out on the couch for the first time after I moved in, I'd twisted the lid off to take a swig.

Vodka.

Should I know that shit at thirteen? Probably not, but I didn't have the luxury of a childhood. Plus, she was always busy covering up the bruises Jerry left on her the mornings after those nights he turned the record player up real loud in their room.

Maybe it was wrong, but since I was already pretty sure I was going to hell since my last foster mom's favorite nickname for me was "spawn of Satan," I was glad of those nights. It meant there was less chance he'd make a move on Destiny.

But Hope? Fuck, Hope meant trouble.

Jerry released them both after the awkwardly long embrace. The social worker was still beaming about her accomplishment of reuniting siblings.

"Well, I'll leave y'all to get better acquainted." She looked at Dixie. "You know the drill. Nothing new."

Jerry laughed, and the bottom of his shirt lifted so his gut hung over his pants. "Nothing but a bump back up in that check we get every month, you mean."

The social worker's smile dimmed a few watts, but she nodded. "Of course." She looked down at the two girls, but focused mostly on the new girl. "You have my number if you need to talk about anything for any reason. I hope you enjoy your new home, and I'm so glad you and Destiny are finally together again."

"She's gonna love it," Jerry said.

As soon as the social worker drove away, Jerry wrapped his sausage-like fingers around Hope's forearm. "I'll show ya your new room. You'll be right next to me and Dixie."

"I can share with Destiny," Hope said. "It's no bother. I don't need my own room."

Jerry ran his tongue over his teeth again. "You're too old to be sharing a room. We got plenty. Come on and don't argue."

That slimy, creepy feeling grew as Jerry dragged her up the stairs, probably headed to the room vacated by another foster kid before Destiny and I showed up within a few days of each other.

From what Jerry Jr. said, that one was a girl too. He was only seven, so he couldn't tell me why she moved on, and I wasn't sure I wanted to know.

Hope's blue eyes, the exact match of Destiny's, locked on me as the trash bag slapped against every step. I saw the fear. She knew she'd just walked into a keg of gunpowder, just waiting for a spark to explode in her face.

I didn't break her stare until they turned the corner at the top of the steps, but I vowed in that moment that if that fat fuck touched her . . . all bets were off.

Hope slept in Destiny's room instead of her own for the first week because Destiny cried whenever Hope left her sight.

Jerry'd had enough of it now. He was drunk and pissed tonight as he slammed his fist on the counter hard enough to make the cheap dishes rattle.

"You stop being a little crybaby. Hope ain't goin' nowhere, and she's sleepin' in her own damn room tonight whether you like it or not."

I'd barely slept all week because I didn't trust him. I was starting to feel drunk from the lack of it, and my schoolwork, which I didn't bother much with anyway, was worse than ever. I'd spent more time in the principal's office than in class since I started at this school. But they expected that from me, from all of us kids in the system. It was like they knew we were set up to fail from day one, so why even try.

All we were was crap.

For me, it was the truth. At least the way I was told, my ma had left me on the stairs of a church in the Quarter and a nun found me, covered in my own shit.

It was a pretty fitting start to how my life had gone. The stain of what I was, *who I was*, followed me everywhere I went.

Sometimes I wondered if my mama had bothered to name me herself before she left me, but it didn't matter. The only name I'd had was the one the nun gave me—Michael. Just as generic as the rest of the bible names they give the thrown-away kids.

"No! Want my sissy!" Destiny cried.

Jerry grabbed her by her thin arm and hauled her closer while reaching for his belt buckle with the other hand. "You want to cry? I'll give you something to cry about."

Hope dropped to her knees in front of her sister, putting her at eye level with Jerry's crotch. "It's okay, Desi. I'll just be a couple rooms away. I'll still be here

7

in the morning when you wake up. I'm not letting them split us up again. I promise."

That promise told me Hope hadn't been in the system as long as I'd thought. If she had, she'd know better than to make any promises. They were all bound to get broken.

Jerry kept his hold on Destiny and his belt buckle, but his attention shifted to Hope. Or rather, down Hope's shirt.

Someone needed to buy the girl a bra, but I guaranteed she wouldn't be getting one from Jerry.

"See, your sister knows how to behave like a good girl." He ran his tongue across his teeth inside his mouth. "*Real* good."

I knew I wouldn't be sleeping again tonight.

Jerry waited until Destiny was asleep and Dixie had passed out in the living room before he made his move. My eyelids were dragged down by what felt like a ton of bricks, but as soon as the old wooden floors creaked, I knew he was on the move.

My blood pumped harder, faster, as I slid out of my doorway and skipped the creaking boards I'd memorized within days of my arrival. Moving silently had its advantages.

The hinges on the door, long since needing oil, squeaked as he pushed it open.

He went toward Hope's bed, and from my position behind him, I saw her bolt up and clutch the covers to her chest like she'd held that trash bag.

Jerry lunged for her, slapping a hand over her mouth. "Don't you fucking scream, or I'll make paying your dues even more taxing, girl."

Hope fought against him, but he shredded her threadbare shirt down the front and her tiny tits fell free. He reached for one and squeezed. His other hand disappeared.

"Get ready to pay your rent, girl. Your sister's too. Unless you want me to take from her. Bet she cries just as pretty as you."

Rage boiled in my empty belly, and I had to force back the urge to puke at his words. He didn't deserve to live.

With the Louisville slugger he'd bought Jerry Jr. for Little League over my shoulder, I flexed my hands, adjusting my grip. I'd take an evil life to save an innocent soul any day of the week.

Jerry ripped back the covers all the way as I stepped through the doorway.

"Don't you fucking touch her."

Jerry whipped around to look at me, and Hope's whimpers of fear filled my ears.

His gaze landed on the bat over my shoulder. "The fuck you think you're gonna do with that, boy? Want me to shove it up your ass since you think you're king shit?"

He moved faster than I would've thought possible, lurching his bulk off the bed and charging me like a bull, his dick swinging out of his dirty pants like a limp hot dog.

That motherfucker.

I didn't think. I swung.

But Jerry ducked, and the bat slammed against the side of his neck. He stumbled backward until he crashed into the wall, his hands going to his throat. He slid to the floor as Hope silently cried in her bed, shaking with fear as she grasped the sheet to cover herself.

Jerry struggled to breathe as I stepped toward him, my disgust growing as I thought about what he would've done to her if I hadn't been here. If he hadn't dodged, I might have crushed his head like a melon with that first swing, but I was glad that didn't happen. He didn't deserve to go that easy or quickly.

A grown man trying to rape a fourteen-year-old girl deserved to die slowly, in as much pain as possible.

I pressed the end of the bat to his hands where they covered whatever I'd hurt in him with my off swing, forcing him to cut off his own air supply as I increased the pressure a little at a time.

"You're never gonna touch another girl in this fucking house."

Jerry's eyes bulged out of his head a little more with every passing second. Finally, for the first time since I stepped foot in this hellhole, I saw fear in them.

It fed into my racing blood, and I didn't hesitate to increase the pressure as he tried to pull his hands free, but couldn't.

He was gonna lose consciousness soon, and I wanted that fear and pain clawing through him before he went. If my suspicions were right, it was no more than what he'd caused plenty of other helpless kids.

"Never again, Jerry. You hear me?"

With as much force as I could, I jammed the bat against his hands, and there was a sharp crunch before I watched the life drain from his eyes.

I gave it another good, hard shove, just to make sure he was really dead. When he slumped to the side, Hope's cries grew louder. I leaned down to check Jerry's pulse.

Nothing. Not a single beat left of his black heart.

I just did the world a favor.

When I stood and met her eyes, the bat dangling from my fingertips, the fear was still there. Except this time, I didn't know who she was more afraid of, but I could probably get it in one guess.

Or maybe I was wrong.

Hope bolted from the bed, the sheet wrapped around her, and slammed into my side. Her arms wrapped around my waist. "Thank you."

I could barely make out the words through her sobs as her tears soaked into my dirty shirt.

"I only did what needed to be done. Now, get dressed and get your shit. I'll get Destiny. You're both getting the fuck out of this house. I'll take you as far as the church shelter a few blocks over. Have them call your social worker. Tell that lady what Jerry tried to do."

She jerked her head around to look at his body. "What do I tell her about . . . this?"

"The truth."

Hope's teary blue gaze lifted to mine, fear in it once more. "But they'll come after you—"

"They'll never find me."

Hope bit her lip and released her grip on me.

"Hurry up. We gotta move."

As soon as I walked out of that house for the last time, both girls huddled behind me, I realized my last foster mom was wrong when she called me the spawn of Satan.

I was the devil himself.

TWO

Mount

Present day

KEIRA PUSHES ME, FRAYING THE EDGES OF MY control, which is something I've never allowed anyone to do.

I fucking slammed a door.

I don't react in anger. Not anymore. All my actions are the result of cold, precise calculation.

But this woman has me slamming fucking doors.

I told myself it wouldn't be a problem. I could have her, keep her, control her—and never let her become anything more than a possession. I promised myself I'd stay detached and indifferent, because the alternative never leads anywhere good. I learned that as a kid.

Treat everything like it's temporary. That's one thing that's always true. None of us make it out of this life alive, so why bother to pretend otherwise?

Another thing I've always thought was true? That

I have complete control over myself and my reactions.

False.

Keira Kilgore has become something I never intended, but I make the rules in my world, so there's nothing fucking stopping me from changing plans now. The best part about being the king? I can do whatever I want.

Keeping her could be a mistake, but I'm not letting her go. Especially now that I have even more hold over her after paying off her bank loans and adding them to her tab.

I've never let myself *want* like this. I may rule an empire, but I've stayed at the top because I've never shown weakness.

She's only a weakness if I allow her to be, and that shit ends right now.

I want to go back to her rooms and tell her exactly how I killed Lloyd Bunt, which would drive her away from me for good.

That's exactly what I should do. But what's the point of ruling an empire if you can't have everything you want, even if you shouldn't have it?

As the thought filters through my brain, I realize I'm on the verge of creating an exploitable weakness. Something I've fought all these years.

But I'm Lachlan fucking Mount. I dragged myself out of the gutters of this unforgiving city, changed my identity, learned to do whatever I needed to not only survive, but *thrive*. I became the weed that grows between the sidewalk cracks and refuses to die. I clawed my way up the ladder of this organization and took the throne by force. To the outside world, I rule through fear, intimidation, and the absolute willingness to back up every single fucking threat I make.

I have every material possession a man could want. At this very moment, I'm walking on white-and-gold Persian carpets between walls plastered by Italian master craftsmen, lit by 14K-gold-plated sconces and crystal chandeliers that cost more than I want to think about. I surround myself with the best of the best, and I don't for one second pretend it's not because I'm still trying to forget what it's like to live in my own filth.

By the time I reach for the hidden latch that releases one of dozens of secret entries leading to a network of passageways connecting every single property I own on this block, I've managed to get my breathing under control.

Every encounter with Keira affects me more than the last, and this one is no exception. I can't let it continue. *I will regain the upper hand.* It's a vow I make as a floor-to-ceiling painting slides aside and leads into the maze.

Other than me, only three other people know every inch of this labyrinth: V, who Keira refers to as Scar; J, my second-in-command; and G, my tailor. All three have proven their loyalty to me time and again, but I'd be naive to ever trust anyone completely.

One thing I've never been is naive.

I take a few turns, barely glancing through the peepholes interspersed along the interior hallway to give me a view of what's happening beyond the walls.

They're impossible to spot unless you know where to look.

Other men in my position would have guards with automatic weapons patrolling the house, but I refuse. First of all, I can fucking handle myself just fine, and second, why allow more possible weak links in my organization? Buying off a low-level guard is too easy. I've done it too many times to count myself. The people I employ can't be bought because they owe me their lives, for one reason or another.

Besides, cameras are more effective, and my security feeds are unhackable . . . or as close as they can be.

When I finish taking the turns and climbing the stairs necessary to reach my inner sanctum, the room J refers to as my lair, I expect the remaining insurrection of emotions roiling through me to be put down as effectively as a revolt.

Not so, because when that fireplace spins and my library comes into view, I know I made a massive mistake thinking this refuge would insulate me from what I'm feeling.

All I can see is *her*. The first night she stood inside these walls, she pulled off that hideous trench coat to reveal her fuckable curves with that ridiculous henna tattoo, and the image is burned in my brain.

She held herself like a queen. Like a woman who could handle the intensity of the king that I have declared myself to be.

No weaknesses, I remind myself again.

My fingers curl into fists, and I'm tempted to put one through the wall. For the first time in longer than I can remember, doubt taunts me.

Maintain control. That's what I do, and I can't let Keira Kilgore change that.

I turn toward the table holding the decanters of liquor and reach for my favorite, only to still my hand in midair.

It's a Seven Sinners whiskey, one I've had my associates appropriate from the distillery's off-site storehouses upon my request, because it's not yet available for sale to the public, except in small batches in the restaurant atop Seven Sinners Distillery, and I'm not a man willing to be denied. I jerk my hand away from the Spirit of New Orleans and reach for the Scotch. After all, my name comes from the Scots. Lachlan Mount sounded like a man who demanded power, and I was fifteen when I chose it.

For the two years I lived on the streets after ending that miserable fuck Jerry's life, I didn't have a name. No one could have cared less about another runaway. The rare nights I slept in shelters, I used a different fake name every time. I lied. I cheated. I stole.

I still do all those things, and what's more, I do them without remorse.

I am not a good man. My soul is black. My heart is stone. My reputation isn't legend or myth, but a collection of facts.

If there were a scale to determine the purity of a person, I would send one side crashing to the ground with the weight of my sins, and laugh while I watched.

I'm going to hell. I know that with full certainty, but there's a long list of people I'll send there ahead of me.

Keira Kilgore is the opposite. She's pure. Innocent. Naive as fuck. She still thinks everyone plays by the rules, and good judgment paves the road to success. She's wrong, but she would never believe me. I never should have brought her into my world, but I'm selfish enough not to care. Selfish enough to keep her here.

"I don't want this. I didn't ask for this, and I will never submit willingly. I swear it on everything that's holy."

She said those words as she stood naked before me, and her body betrayed her. I made a liar out of her too because every time I took her, she was more than willing. She wanted it as badly as I did.

I swear I can smell her in this room over the leather, old books, and cigar smoke, and it makes me want to stalk back to her room, rip open the door, and make a liar out of her again.

"Don't you dare fucking touch me right now. Or ever again."

She should know better than to throw down the gauntlet with a man like me. I win every time.

I clench my teeth and force myself to walk toward a bookshelf like there's a chance in hell I'm going to read one of the volumes on it.

A whoosh signals the swivel of the fireplace entrance, and I spin around. I almost expect an enraged red-haired goddess, come to take me to task again. Which, in my filthy mind, would end with her bent over the arm of one of my chairs, me fucking her with her hands pinned behind her back.

But it's not. It's J, my second-in-command.

"We've got an issue, a sensitive one. I'd handle it myself, but I know you'll want input."

"What?" I ask, glad for the distraction.

"Lieutenant to one of the cartel jefes has already been warned once about the way he's handling his girl for the night on the gaming-room floor, but the dumb fuck isn't getting the message."

The familiar coldness of purpose settles over me, bringing me back to center. This is where I excel. Something I can easily control.

J's right. This isn't a situation that needs my assistance, but I do want input. And tonight . . . maybe I'll even handle it myself.

"Let's go."

I follow J as we leave my study and all reminders of Keira. We head back through the rabbit warren of passageways to the casino floor. Owning an entire block of the French Quarter has its perks, like being able to remove interior walls and turn the center section of half the block into an underground gambling establishment that produces more profit in a night than most men make in a year. Membership is exclusive, selective, and rarely granted. Only the very rich, very powerful, or very well-connected are allowed in, with the unspoken threat hanging over all their heads—if you talk, you die. If you cheat, you die. If you look at me wrong, you die.

When I say I rule over them with intimidation and fear, backed up by action, there is no exaggeration.

We arrive through the rear club entrance I always use, and it takes only moments to locate the private room where the lieutenant with a death wish is now playing high-stakes blackjack.

The girls who work this club are under my protection, and an offense against them is an offense against me. I don't care that their dresses barely cover their tits, pussies, or asses, or that their makeup is thicker than the paint on my favorite car. It doesn't matter that they're working for their money in the world's oldest profession. They don't get manhandled in my club. That's part of the rules, but drunk men sometimes forget. When they do, I have no problem with my staff reminding them of the consequences.

This girl, a skinny blonde with dark roots, is trying to discreetly disentangle herself from his embrace, attempting to avoid a scene. The dumb fuck, as J called him, isn't letting her free. Instead, he fists her hair and yanks her down with such force, she hits her knees.

My phone vibrates in my pocket, but I ignore it as wrath fills my veins. The ones who fuck with the blondes always bring it out of me even more.

The lieutenant, who is at least six inches shorter than me and fifty pounds lighter, forces her face into his lap. "Suck my dick, bitch."

"He dies tonight." I say it quietly, but J doesn't ask me to repeat myself. This is a foregone conclusion.

"I'll take care of it, boss."

I shake my head as I harness my rage and turn it cold. "No. I'm handling this personally."

"You sure? I can—"

When I swing my stare to J, my second-in-command sucks in a breath.

"Of course you're sure. Maybe it'll be better coming from you anyway."

J assumes I'm doing this myself because it'll send a clear message to the lieutenant's jefe, but that's only part of it. Tonight, I need an outlet for everything raging inside me, and this piece of shit picked the wrong day and the wrong motherfucker's place to cause problems. He won't make that mistake again.

I stride into the room, drawing the attention of the three other players and the dealer as soon as I close the door behind me with a decisive click.

The dealer will never speak of what he sees in this room because he owes me his life. I stopped him from being murdered execution-style on a street corner by a crack dealer when he was sixteen. He also knows that breathing a word of what happens here would be a betrayal resulting in the same fate he escaped. Besides, he makes a healthy living, has a pregnant girlfriend that he's planning to marry next month, and wouldn't dare put her and the baby in jeopardy.

The other players are a dirty city councilman, a megachurch preacher, and an oil baron who has ruthlessly driven people out of their homes to expand his territory. With the dirt I have on each of them, they wouldn't dare talk either.

As I cross the room, I don't speak. Actions carry more power than words, and power is what I know. I stop a foot behind the lieutenant's chair and grab him by the black braid at the base of his skull. I wrap it around my hand and, with a yank, jerk his head backward until his neck is overextended. His Adam's apple bobs in his throat.

When he drops his hold on the girl's hair, I rip him out of his chair and drag him over the back of it. Using his braid as a rope, I lift him off his feet, watching them dangle inches above the floor as his expression morphs into shock.

I may be over forty, but I push my workouts to the max every day. I learned firsthand too damn young that sometimes brute strength is all that stands between you and your worst nightmare.

The skin of his scalp stretches until a chunk of his braid rips free, leaving a bloody patch of skin attached to the hair in my hand. His feet hit the floor first, but his legs give out and he drops to his knees in front of me.

Exactly where he belongs.

A stream of unintelligible Spanish follows, but it doesn't matter what he says. No one crosses the line here, no exceptions.

He puts both palms on the floor, ready to jump up. *Not happening.* Before he can move, I slam a heel down on the hand that he used to touch her, crushing the bones beneath my handmade Italian shoes.

His pathetic scream won't leave the room because of the soundproof walls and door.

I look at the girl, taking in the red marks that circle her throat from where he must have grabbed her before I arrived. Disgusted, I toss the braid on the floor in front of him.

I believe in street justice. Not only an eye for an eye, but that retribution comes threefold. When I grab him the second time, it's by the throat, and I drag him toward the wall and lift again until his spine slams into it.

He tries to speak, but the pressure on his windpipe makes it impossible. His eyes bulge, finally showing a hint of fear, and I'm taken back to that night. The night that ultimately forged the man I am today. The call girl on the floor becomes Hope, and this piece of shit is the sick fuck who tried to rape her.

I release my hold for a moment, ignoring the constant buzzing of my phone in my left pocket as I reach into the right and slip my fingers into an accessory I'm rarely without.

He catches his breath, his hand cradled in front of him, and the begging in Spanish comes again. He should save his breath. He's not walking out of here tonight, and everyone in this room knows it.

When I remove my hand from my pocket, my fingers curl into a fist around my 24K-gold-plated brass knuckles. I pull back and deliver a single punch to his throat, crushing his windpipe and snapping his neck. The raised letters on the brass knuckles leave an impression: Mount.

His body slides to the floor as I step back and return my knuckles to my pocket, flexing my hand.

"Have someone take out the trash," I tell J before I reach for the door handle and pause.

I turn, meeting the horrified stares of each person in the room. I have no doubt they feel the brutality emanating from me, and I will have no problems resulting from this night. If anything, my legend and their fear will grow.

Satisfied, I open the door to the main room and shut it behind me before finally reaching into my pocket to pull out my phone.

I have eight texts from V, and six missed calls from the control center.

THREE

Mount

"**W**HERE THE FUCK IS SHE?"

"Her apartment. She got out, and somehow we missed it because . . . well . . . we were watching what was happening in the black-jack room. But we started trying to reach you as soon as we realized it," L, one of the control-room staff explains over the phone. "V is on his way there already. He wouldn't wait."

V's getting a motherfucking raise.

"What the fuck happened? How did she get out without you seeing?"

L doesn't dance around the issue; he knows I accept no excuses. "We fucked up, boss. Didn't have her tracker up on-screen because she hasn't tried to run. Didn't expect her to try."

"I'll deal with you later," I grind out, and disconnect the call.

25

Nothing matters right now but Keira.

I don't read the eight texts from V, but I guarantee between those and the missed calls from the control room, I would have known she was gone a lot fucking sooner if I hadn't been finding an outlet for my frustration that didn't include fucking her into submission.

I head to the garage where a few of my cars are kept and grab the keys to the Porsche 918 Spyder. I'm not fucking around, and it's the fastest car I own at the moment.

The engine is already revving when I press a button on the steering wheel, accessing a private camera feed only I have access to. When it flickers to life on the small dashboard screen, I press the button again, toggling through various feeds until it shows Keira in her apartment's bedroom. I wait for a few minutes and watch as she finds the box and flings it against the wall, cursing me. And then curses me again when she realizes what's inside.

I knew a day would come when she'd escape or I'd let her return to her apartment. I've wanted to tell her a hundred times that it was me that night at the masquerade, but I knew it wouldn't make her hate me any less. So, why did I leave the evidence? Because part of me has always wanted her to know the truth.

The fact that I thought she was waiting for *me* and not that fuckwad Brett still burns.

The engine roars and the tires of the Spyder roast as I tear out of the garage and onto the empty street. I know the fastest route to her apartment easily, because I've driven it more times than I would ever admit over the last several months.

I may be a brutal man, but one thing I've learned over the years is that patience is its own reward. Obtaining Keira has been the ultimate exercise in that lesson.

I swerve around random pedestrians and run a red light, yanking the steering wheel and cursing as the rear end breaks loose as I round a corner. Keeping one eye on the road as I drive like a man possessed, I continue to monitor the screen until she leaves the bedroom, and I tap the button to switch over to the living-room camera feed.

I floor the accelerator, the engine screaming through the streets, at what I see. Brett Hyde, that worthless piece of shit, has come back from the dead.

One thing I know with absolute certainty—his new lease on life won't last long.

FOUR

Keira

THE DOOR TO MY APARTMENT FLIES OPEN AGAIN for the second time tonight. I spin around as the dim light of the hallway spills into my living room where I've been pacing back and forth in the dark, a butcher knife clutched in my right hand and a hammer in the left.

Brett had a gun. I didn't. We all know who wins in that equation. But he didn't shoot me because, apparently, he doesn't want me dead. No, I'm more useful to him alive.

My sight blurs with tears at what I'm about to do, but it doesn't stop my banshee battle cry as I rush toward the shadowy intruder, the knife above my head and the hammer swinging. The knife is batted away and clatters to the floor, but the hammer connects. He grunts before ripping it from my hands. It lands with a thud as I'm flipped around to face the wall and my wrists are grasped and pinned against my hips. A hard chest slams into my back as I'm pressed against the peeling paint. I jerk and attempt to yank away, but he has me in a human straitjacket.

"Let me go, you motherfucker! I already said I would do it. If you hurt my parents or my sisters, I'll kill you with my bare hands."

Instead of Brett's smarmy voice in my ear, all I hear is a grunt. I breathe in, and the scent coming off the man holding me captive isn't the one that haunts my past *and* my present. But the grunt is familiar.

"Let me go!" I demand again, and he gives my wrists a shake.

I blink back the tears in my eyes as I crane my head around, almost afraid to see if I'm right. Scar's profile is visible in the watery wash of light.

A sense of relief I probably shouldn't feel while in the arms of the man who has been instrumental in keeping me captive sweeps through me, and I stop struggling. My lungs still heave, but my body relaxes a few degrees.

"Let me go. I won't run. Or kill you. Probably. Maybe." At this point, I don't know what I'm capable of. Definitely more than I ever thought possible.

Scar waits several beats before releasing his hold on my wrists. I spin around, rubbing the spots where his hands shackled mine as I back away, never taking my eyes off his face. When the back of my knees hit the couch, I collapse. Tremors rock my body, and I wrap my arms around my middle like I'm holding myself together.

"He didn't even bother to come himself?" My voice shakes like the rest of me, and I'm pissed off that I care that it's not Mount I almost killed. "I shouldn't be surprised. I'm not important enough for him to leave his little fortress."

Scar doesn't respond verbally. Instead, he reaches into his pocket and pulls out his phone. He types something into it, and a few seconds later, his fingers fly again.

From the table across the room, my phone dings with a text, and my eyes lock on Scar. He jerks his chin toward it.

I stand, my knees still wobbly as I cross the room to snatch it up and find a text waiting for me.

UNKNOWN NUMBER: *Boss is on his way.*

My gaze lifts to Scar. Instead of the information calming me, it creates a firestorm of emotions inside me, springing from the vivid flashback spawned by the discovery of my note and the thong I wore to the Mardi Gras ball. Mount expected me to learn the truth all along, the manipulative bastard. Maybe not this soon, but eventually.

"Did you know about his plan all along?" When I think about all the things Brett told me before he left, my temper burns hotter and faster.

Scar's expression goes blank, and he doesn't move to type a response. Instead, he flips on the lights I turned off as soon as my not-so-dead husband left, worried Brett would come back. I wanted every advantage I

30

could get if I had the opportunity to take him on.

"I hate both of you," I say to Scar, conviction backing each word like steel plating.

For the next several minutes, I sit in silence because there's no point in asking more questions I know won't be answered. With each passing second, my shoulders tense and my spine straightens in preparation for the inevitable confrontation.

Mount is coming. It's only a matter of time.

Footsteps thunder down the hall as if someone's running, and my apartment door crashes open again.

His black eyes burning and chest heaving, Mount stands in my doorway looking like he's ready to commit murder.

I don't think before I act. I launch off the couch and fly across the room until I collide with him. His arms move to wrap around me, but I'm not seeking comfort. Not from him.

My hands curl into fists as I beat against his solid chest. The tears I've been struggling to hold back all night flow in rivers down my cheeks.

"How could you do this to me, you bastard? This is my life, not a game! How much do you have to hate someone to do this to them?"

I pound on him hard enough to leave bruises, but he doesn't stop me. My arms burn and the impact lessens with each strike until my voice, hoarse with emotion, quiets to a whisper.

"Why me? Why not someone else? Anyone else?"

I drop my forehead against Mount's chest, not caring that I'm soaking his shirt with my tears. It's a torrent, but I feel no shame. This man was responsible for turning my life upside down before I even knew he existed.

One of his strong arms wraps around my waist and his free hand cradles the back of my head, pressing it against his chest. "Shhhh."

"Don't tell me to *shhhh*." My shaky response is weak but still snappish.

"My little Irish hellion. You'll fight to your last breath."

"So would you."

Something presses against the top of my head, and I think it's his chin.

"You're finally starting to understand." He keeps his tone quiet and steady, but his words set me off again.

I shove both palms against his chest and he drops his hold on me, *allowing* me to go free.

I'm under no illusions anymore. Nothing in my life happens without his permission. Well, almost nothing.

"I don't understand *anything*, obviously, because if I did, I wouldn't have seen a ghost tonight when my dead husband showed up at my door."

Mount's expression, which for a flash of a moment held something soft, hardens. "He was supposed to stay dead."

I take another step back in the direction of my bedroom and cross my arms over my chest. "He said you paid him. The loan that you used as leverage on me, he said you gave him that money on the condition that he'd disappear. He said you faked his death! Is that true?"

"Yes." Mount steps toward me without a hint of remorse in his expression.

Tremors threaten my body again as he comes closer. I swallow, not sure I want to ask the next question, because I already know the answer. But some stupid part of me needs to hear him admit the truth.

"That night, at the masquerade, when I wrote that note for Brett to come, it was really you, wasn't it?"

He takes another step toward me. "Yes."

My hands clench into fists. "Why? How could you do that knowing I thought it was him?"

Mount's expression, already hard, turns to granite. The muscle in his jaw ticks. "I thought you knew it was me."

"That's impossible." The answer comes out on a stunned breath.

His dark eyes narrow as he shakes his head. "*I* got your note. Not Brett. I assumed you were instructed to write it. I thought it was part of the game, and you were the gift left for me."

I haul back in shock at his words. "A *gift*? Like you're some kind of warlord people deliver women to as prizes?"

Instead of answering my question, Mount turns to look at Scar and jerks his head toward my apartment door. "Wait outside. Make sure we're secure. Handle any threats."

"What—"

I don't even have a chance to form a question before Mount prowls forward, stalking me until we're in my bedroom. He kicks the door shut behind him.

I'm trapped in my room with the man who thought I'd been given to him as a gift.

And to top it off, my dead husband isn't dead.

Nothing makes sense anymore, especially the fact that I'm more scared of the man I married than the brutal stranger towering over me.

FIVE

Mount

"TELL ME EVERYTHING."

My words are a razor-sharp demand as I turn on the light. Seeing her in this shithole apartment, shaking in fear, fuels my rage against the man who never should have gotten close to her again.

Hours ago, she was perfectly dressed in designer clothes, defying me like an empress, and now her hair is tangled in her face and her eyes are red from crying. All because of him.

If he fucking touched her . . .

Keira laughs, a harsh edge breaking through. Instead of bouncing off the walls, the sound is absorbed by cracked drywall and peeling paint. Her ceiling fan clicks as it rotates while I wait for her to respond. She wraps her arms around her middle, and I wonder how close she is to her breaking point.

"Don't you know *everything*?" she snaps back.

I whip my phone from my pocket and hold the

screen toward her. The secured website only I can access with the camera footage of her apartment and rooms in my home is up on the screen, just as it was in my Spyder as I broke every law to get here as fast as possible.

Keira jerks her head back. "What is that?"

"Video feed. I can either watch the rest or you can tell me what happened. Either way, I'm getting every detail. Now tell me, did he fucking touch you?"

Fury blazes in her green gaze. "How *dare* you invade my privacy? Where are the cameras?"

"*Did he touch you*?" My question comes out as a dull roar, but in this neighborhood, the residents wouldn't dare interfere.

I wait for her answer, ready to repeat it again. I have to know. I have to hear it from her.

Her jaw muscle ticks before she replies. "No, he didn't touch me. He doesn't want me! He never wanted me. No one does."

"That's where you're wrong."

That hard-edged laugh of hers grates on my nerves before she speaks once more. "I'm just a game to you."

Her words are fuel on the fire already burning in me.

"You don't have a goddamned clue what you are to me. You don't know a fucking thing."

"Bullshit." The word is a challenge, and her green eyes flash like emeralds before she continues. "I bet right now all you want to do is beat me until I tell you everything you want to know."

I move toward her, one measured step at a time,

until her spine touches the wall directly across from the door of her tiny bedroom.

"Wrong. I want to spank your ass for putting yourself at risk, and then I want to fuck the hell out of you so there's no question in your mind about whether I want you. Maybe then you'll finally realize who you belong to."

Her nostrils flare. "I don't belong to anyone. I'm not a goddamned dog."

"No, but you're still fucking *mine*."

Her hand flings out just before her palm cracks across my cheek.

SIX

Keira

Holy shit. I slapped him. I actually slapped him.

Before I can snatch my hand back, Mount captures my wrist.

"Only you would dare." His voice rumbles even deeper than before as I attempt to dart around him, but he snatches my other hand and pins them both against the wall over my head. "Fucking hellion."

His declaration from moments before roars through my mind like a freight train at top speed.

"I want to spank your ass for putting yourself at risk, and then I want to fuck the hell out of you so there's no question in your mind about whether I want you. Maybe then you'll finally realize who you belong to."

I should be feeling terror as this brutal man pins me against the wall, but raw emotion claws at my insides, and it has nothing to do with fear. No, it's anticipation at the thought of him following through on his threat.

He's turning me into someone I don't recognize.

"Let me go." I voice the demand, but there's no power behind it.

He lowers his face to mine and whispers a single word. "*Never.*"

Mount's mouth collides with mine, his teeth closing over my bottom lip and tugging at it with a sharp nip. When my tongue slips out to soothe it, he steals inside, angling his head to gain better access.

The kiss is pure chaos. A wild, angry tempest of a storm. It strips away all my inhibitions and sparks a recklessness in me I don't recognize.

With my wrists pinned over my head and his chest pressed against mine, he owns my mouth, taking it over and over with certainty, but completely lacking in the clever skill I would have expected. This is no tried-and-true move he's cultivated over the years. This is something completely unpracticed and unhinged.

I said I'd never kiss him. What the hell am I doing? He's breaking all my rules. Stealing every bit of my control over my body and my emotions. *How can he do this to me?* I can't pretend I don't want it. Want him.

Before I realize what's happening, Mount tears us away from the wall and backs me up against my bed before we both topple onto it. His heavy weight lands on me, sending a feeling of satisfaction screaming through my blood.

I struggle, tugging at his grip, but I'm not seeking freedom from him. I want the freedom to *touch* him. I want to bury my fingernails in his shoulders again, uncaring that my brain has lost its capacity for rational thought in favor of this animalistic craving.

He tears his mouth from mine, looking as crazed as I feel. "Tell me you want this as bad as I do."

I wet my lower lip, loving the sting his teeth left behind, as I pretend to pull myself together. One coherent thought breaks through the primitive need firing in my blood, and I pull back an inch so I can see his face clearly.

"You have to promise me something first."

He says nothing as his dark gaze drinks in my features. His pulse pounds in his throat as his lungs heave. The scent that I remember all too well wafts over me. Finally, his eyes lock on mine.

"Promise you won't let anything happen to my family. You won't let Brett or anyone else hurt them. Ever."

The muscle in his jaw ticks, but he pauses only a single beat before replying. "Done."

His lips crash against mine again and I pry my hands free, grasping his shoulders and lifting my hips to press against the bulging hard-on barely contained by his suit pants. My new piercing sends jolts of sensation streaking through my body.

"You make me fucking crazy," he says on a breath as he reaches down to capture one breast in his big palm, teasing the nipple into a taut peak through my blouse before pinching it between his thumb and forefinger.

Pleasure rushes from my nipple to my center, and I buck harder against him. I let out a moan because, *holy hell*, it feels more incredible than ever.

He releases my nipple and lifts up just long enough to shove my skirt up my body and tear my thong free with a single snap of the lace band. I tense, expecting the next onslaught, but he goes still.

"Say it."

My mind, devoid of rational thought, can't grasp the question. "What?" I ask, looking into his intense face.

"Tell me you want this. Right here. Right now."

I lift up, again seeking pressure, but he holds me down with a hand wrapped around my hip.

"Please—" I stop short because I don't want to beg.

"Please what?"

"Fuck me!"

Much like he had the night he shattered the dishes and crystal in the dining room by sweeping them off the table, my command unleashes Mount's primal nature.

"Thank Christ."

His fingers find my center, already soaked, and he plunges one inside.

It's not enough. I need more. I want his touch on my clit and the heightened sensation from my new jewelry. And then I want his hard cock filling me.

"More."

His dark eyes blaze with possession. "I'll give you every fucking thing you need."

He thumbs the jewel at my clit as he finger-fucks me to the verge of orgasm, stopping just before I fly over the edge.

"No!"

Mount rips off his belt and releases the button on his pants before tearing down his zipper. His cock springs free between us and he fists it with one big hand, giving it a hard tug. "Don't you tell me no."

"Fuck you!"

He shakes his head as a wicked smile curves across his lips. He jacks his cock again before positioning the head against my opening. "No, Keira, I'm the one fucking you. The *only one.*"

I buck upward, trying to seize control of this power struggle and force him inside, but his hand prevents me from getting more than just the tip.

"Tell me you want my cock. Only mine." He growls the demand through clenched teeth, like his grip on his sanity is slipping as fast as mine.

"Yes! Give it to me!"

With a roar, he buries himself inside me. He releases one of my wrists but keeps the other pinned over my head. As he drives into me, his mouth finds mine again, taking more than I ever expected to give, and giving me back something I never knew I needed.

His dominance is unquestionable as he powers inside over and over, each stroke giving me exactly the friction I need on my piercing to come.

"Not yet," he orders.

"I can't wait."

"Yes. You. Will."

Each word is punctuated by a thrust, but no matter what he says, I can't stop myself from coming. I scream, his cock pulsing inside me as his orgasm is torn from his body at the same time as mine.

His one hand stays clamped around my hip, and his heart pounds in his chest hard enough to reverberate through my entire body. A bead of sweat from his forehead lands on my chin and slides down my neck.

I don't know what happened in this room, but for the span of time it lasted, the only person who existed in my world was Mount. Everything and everyone else fell away.

Finally, he releases my wrist. I draw it to my chest, wrapping my fingers around where he gripped it.

"You hurt?"

I shake my head and whisper, "No."

His forehead lowers toward mine, filling my lungs with his unique, addictive scent. "I swear I thought you knew it was me that night at the masquerade."

The change of subject drags me out of this refuge and into reality with a cruel, abrupt jolt.

"How could you have possibly thought I wanted *you*—"

Before I can finish my sentence, his expression shutters, going completely blank before he levers himself off my body.

I was going to add *because I didn't even know you existed,* but he's already out of sight and my bathroom door slams behind him. I hear the toilet flush and then the taps turn on.

Moments later, Mount fills the bathroom doorway, his pants zipped and his shirt tucked in. His features are as forbidding as they've ever been. If I hadn't been under him only minutes ago, my lips still bruised from his mouth, I'd have no clue he was the same man who just made me scream in ecstasy. His face is that horrible mask of granite. He's completely shut down.

"Get yourself cleaned up. We're leaving, and you still have a story to tell me."

SEVEN

Mount

WE RIDE BACK TO THE HOUSE IN STRAINED silence. I almost had V take her, but I'm not ready to let her out of my sight. I'm also determined to get the answers I want before this night is over.

At least three times, Keira opens her mouth like she's going to say something, but she snaps it shut before a single word comes out. Neither of us is willing to give an inch. If I do, she'll take a mile, and if she does, I'll take a thousand.

When I make the final turn, V's headlights flash behind me, indicating that he's pulling into the garage where a few of the other cars are parked.

"You're actually going to let me see where you live?" she asks, surprise in her tone.

"It's not like it's much of a secret now that you've escaped," I say, and catch her pursing her lips in my peripheral vision.

"True." Quietly, she adds, "But I kind of wish I hadn't."

Her confession shocks me, but instead of showing any reaction, I focus on parking and getting the fuck out of the car before the smell of sex on her body drives me any more insane than I obviously already am.

I park the Spyder next to a McLaren and a Ferrari and kill the engine. With the garage door shutting behind us, I'm done waiting.

"Tell me every goddamn word he said to you."

Instead of protesting like the hellion I've become accustomed to, Keira sighs. "I'm going to need a drink for this."

I open the door and the dome light illuminates, giving me a better view of her face than the garage fixtures alone. Her expression is hard to decipher. Sated, defeated, yet defiant. Every time I think I have her figured out, I realize none of my normal barometers apply when it comes to Keira Kilgore. She's the exception to everything I thought I knew.

"Let's go."

I climb out of the car, and she's still trying to find the latch to open hers when I round the hood and open it for her, grasping her by the hand to pull her out.

"Stupid fancy cars."

"Says the girl with one that barely runs."

Her shoulders stiffen at the insult. "Sorry, I don't have a bazillion dollars of dirty money to build a super-car collection."

"You make your money feeding people's addictions. How is it any different from what I do? We're both in the business of sin, just in different ways."

"I don't even know what the hell you really do. And don't make me sound like a drug dealer. My business is perfectly legal." Her chin lifts with her condescending tone.

Rather than address the part of her comment about not knowing what I really do—because that's something I have no plans to ever tell her—I focus on the one thing she can't deny.

"Tell me alcoholism can't be just as destructive as drug addiction."

"It's different!"

"Keep telling yourself that, sweetheart, but get off your high horse once in a while to acknowledge that what you do isn't pure and innocent either."

She snaps her mouth closed, and I assume it's because she doesn't have a reply. Again, I'm wrong.

"Take me to the booze. You better have the good stuff."

I think of the whiskey I almost drank earlier but wouldn't, because I didn't want to feed into my obsession with her. That goal is well and truly fucked after tonight.

"I have the best of everything, and that includes liquor."

I wrap my hand around hers and pull her to a secret door in the garage that leads into the network of internal hallways, rather than going by way of the normal entrance.

She tries to tug her hand away, but my grip is stronger. Eventually, she stops fighting in favor of asking questions.

"How much did it cost to build all these? Or were they already here? Are those peepholes? Oh my God, do you have peepholes into my room?" Abruptly, she stops moving, forcing me to a halt.

I turn halfway, just enough to meet her horrified gaze. "Why would I need peepholes when I have cameras on every angle of your rooms?"

Her mouth drops open and she sucks in an outraged breath. "I can't believe you let people watch me! Us!" She lifts her free hand like she's going to slap me again, but I snag it in midair, which is turning out to be a handy skill with this fiery redhead.

"You got in your only free shot tonight. The next time you try to hit me, I'll take it out on your ass, tenfold. Actions have consequences. Especially if there are other eyes watching."

I'm not sure which part of what I said finally penetrates, but her hand goes slack.

"Do you really think I'd let anyone see your tits, your ass, or your pussy? You're *mine*, and I don't fucking share. No one has access to those feeds but me. The control room only watches your tracker on GPS, and when they alerted me, I pulled the private camera feeds."

Her head jerks back again. "Tracker? I'm wearing a tracking device?" Her voice rises another octave as she pats down her clothes, all of which have been supplied by my people. When her fingers touch the necklace chain, her mouth drops open. "It's not just a lock, is it? You chipped me like a damn dog."

"Quit referring to yourself as a dog. You might act like a bitch sometimes, but you're sure as fuck not as obedient as one. Be fucking grateful I had that tonight. What else could've happened to you if V and I hadn't gotten there?"

When she yanks at the chain until it threatens to break her skin, I close my fingers over hers, stilling her movement. "Leave it alone. It's not coming off."

Her gaze burns into mine, and I can see the words she wants to speak but has been forbidden from uttering. *I hate you.*

At least she's learning.

We reach the hidden library entrance, and I pull her against my chest.

"Let me go."

She struggles against me, but I squeeze tighter. "Shut up, Keira."

The platform spins, and I release her as soon as we're in the library.

She darts across the room as if she can't get away from me fast enough.

Try all you want, hellion. It won't work.

She stops in front of the sideboard with the crystal decanters, not waiting to be served.

Lifting the stopper from one decanter, she sniffs it and wrinkles her nose, then unstops another bottle and inhales. She repeats the process until she whirls around to face me, and I know exactly which decanter is gripped in her hand.

"How did you get Spirit of New Orleans? You can only get it in our restaurant, and I sure as hell didn't send you one of the promotional bottles."

I give her a look that can only be interpreted as *Are you seriously asking me that question?*

Keira rolls her eyes. "When I find out who got it for you, I'm going to have to fire them. You know that, right?"

My laugh booms out, surprising us both. "Like I need inside help. You, on the other hand, need to upgrade security at your storehouses."

Pure shock flashes across her features. "You stole a barrel of my best whiskey? How dare—"

I stride across the room, stopping a foot from her. "I dare whatever the fuck I please. One of these days, you'll figure that out."

A growl escapes her throat as she turns around and pours herself a tumbler before tossing it back. "You're—"

I close the gap between us and press my palms to the wood on either side of her, trapping her against my body. Her spine stiffens when my chest touches her back.

"What am I, Keira? Tell me." My lips almost brush her ear.

She releases another growl of frustration, and I want to fucking devour her. "Impossible. You're impossible."

With a smirk on my lips, I drop my nose to the curve where her shoulder and neck meet, and inhale. "And you smell like me and filthy, incredible sex. Now, pour me a fucking drink and tell me what the hell happened."

I'll give her credit—her hand doesn't shake as she pours three fingers into her glass and another. I step away and wait for her to turn around. When she does, any shock from my words has been wiped clean from her face.

Impressive.

I accept the tumbler she holds out as she sips her own, closing her eyes to appreciate the flavor, and I force myself to look away before I get a hard-on just from watching her drink.

She lowers the tumbler from her lips and speaks like the few moments before didn't happen. Again, I'm impressed at how unaffected she's able to make herself sound.

"I always forget how good this is. I swear I could drink a bottle myself." When I narrow my gaze on her, she rolls her eyes. "You do realize I was practically raised on whiskey. I'm no lightweight."

"You're not drinking an entire bottle tonight." I move back to lean against one of the chairs, set my glass down untouched, and cross my arms. "You're telling me what that piece of shit said."

A small, sad smile plays over her lips as she stares down into the whiskey. "Funny, that's one thing we actually agree on. Brett Hyde is a piece of shit." She looks up from her glass, her green eyes stormy. "He threatened my parents. He said if I don't follow his instructions, he'll have them and my sisters killed."

I recall the picture I had taken of her parents while I was leaving reminders of everything she had to lose in order to make her accept my bargain. "And you think he can pull it off?"

"Maybe not, but I gave myself up to you to protect them. What makes you think I won't take him seriously?"

Uncrossing my arms, I reach for the tumbler to finally take a drink of the whiskey. "What instructions did he give you?"

"I'm supposed to go to the bank tomorrow and make a large cash withdrawal. The biggest I can without my father's approval."

My fingers grip the crystal almost tightly enough to shatter it. *That greedy motherfucker.*

"How did he know you had cash in the account?"

She shrugs. "I didn't even know I had it until he showed me the balance on his phone with the online banking app. I didn't think about shutting down his access *because I thought he was dead.*" Her last words are tossed at me like an accusation as her eyes narrow. "Don't think I'm not pissed about you trying to force me deeper into your debt. That's bullshit. I didn't ask for that money. I didn't ask for any of this."

I pinch the bridge of my nose with my thumb and forefinger. "I loaned you operating capital so you can make the next payroll. That check from the Voodoo Kings for the event deposit won't come until days after you need it. Or did you want your employees' paychecks to bounce?"

The color drains from her face. "How do you know that?"

"When it comes to you and your business, I know *everything.*"

"Except, apparently, that my dead husband wouldn't stay dead." She turns her back on me and begins to pace, which I've come to realize is one of her habits. "Why would I think to disable his bank access when he died? He was *dead,* so it wasn't like I was worried he was going to try to steal from the distillery." She spins as she hits the end of her path and spears me with her furious green gaze. "But he wasn't dead, and I wish I would've known that so I could have prevented him from getting an alert when our balance tipped a certain number. Because I didn't know he could do that either."

Once a con, always a con. I'm actually surprised Brett was smart enough to work this one. He signed his death warrant when he showed his face again, and this time, it's going to be even more painful. Not just because of what he put Keira through tonight, but since the day she married him.

"Why didn't he ask you to wire it to an offshore account? That would've been smarter. He's a dumb motherfucker, but not that stupid. A cash withdrawal leaves way too many variables that could go wrong."

She turns to pace again, dumping the remains of the whiskey down her throat as she strides along the wood floor. "I don't have wire transfer authority and neither does Brett. Only my father does, and there's no way in hell I could have explained to him that I needed to wire money into an offshore account. Do you realize the questions that would've led to? The least of which being how the hell I even got my hands on that much money?" When she comes back toward me, the strong front she's been holding together cracks, and so does her voice. "But he said he'd kill them all if I don't do it, so I don't have a choice. I'm going to the bank tomorrow morning, and then, God willing, it'll be over."

I lower my glass to the table and step into her path, forcing her to stop and look up at me when I wrap a hand around each of her shoulders.

"Give him that money, and he'll keep coming back for more. That's how this works."

"Then what the hell do I do? I can't let my family suffer for my bad decision."

I tighten my grip on her to make sure I have her complete attention. When she meets my gaze, I repeat the promise I made earlier. "No one will touch them."

"Swear it to me."

"I already did."

"I need to hear it again."

I give her a squeeze. "I don't repeat myself."

She bites her lip, and I'd give a hell of a lot to know what she's thinking.

"Fine. But if you don't, all bets are off."

"You don't make that decision. But I will make you one more promise—Brett Hyde might be back from the dead, but it won't be long before you're a widow again."

EIGHT

Keira

MOUNT LEADS ME OUT OF THE STUDY AFTER prying the whiskey glass from my fingers. I still can't believe he managed to steal a barrel of the Spirit of New Orleans from one of Seven Sinners' rackhouses. It's not like a serious security upgrade is part of the budget right now either. I'm too busy mulling over this problem to notice that the hallways we travel aren't the same ones I've been down before.

When Mount pushes open one massive black double door, I take a step inside and stop.

"This isn't my room. I mean, my *cell*."

Where the decor I'd been surrounded by before was utterly feminine, this is the polar opposite, even though it's the same color scheme. Mount's masculine stamp is on every detail, from the soaring glossy black ceilings that are well over three times my height, to the matching thick black molding. An enormous black leather sectional sofa takes up the middle of the sitting room, across from a massive flat-screen TV that looks like it recesses into the wall to be hidden. The coffee table is also black lacquer with gold accents. A black-and-gold liquor cabinet holds more booze than the one in his library.

That may have been his escape, but this is Mount's home. This is where he lives, where no one sees him. His scent pervades the room, getting stronger as I take a few more steps toward the next set of double doors. I peek inside to see a bedroom.

The bed is the largest one I've ever seen. It could sleep part of the Voodoo Kings and still have room for a few cheerleaders. The spread is black velvet, edged in gold, with black sheets and pillows.

"Do you like any colors other than black, white, and gold?"

Mount studies me as I explore his sanctuary. "No."

I step back from the doorway, the ache between my legs telling me I don't need to get too close to that bed, or there's no telling what might happen.

Mount is turning me into an addict, stripping me of control of my own body and compelling me to hand it over willingly at the same time. It's a paradox, one I don't want to contemplate any more tonight. I step away from the bedroom.

All that matters right now is figuring out how I'm going to pull off the bank withdrawal Brett demanded, get him the money, and escape unscathed.

"Okay, so I'm going to need my trench coat, dark sunglasses, and a duffel bag. Preferably with some of those packets that explode dye in someone's face so he can't spend a damned dollar of it." I'm already pacing Mount's living room, something I find myself doing all too often lately. "And definitely a gun. I've been to the range a couple times, and I'm pretty sure I'd have no problem pulling the trigger if Brett waves his in my face again."

Up until that moment, Mount has been content to let me ramble, but at that last sentence, he strides toward me and snags my elbow in his grip. "He held a gun on you?"

I nod.

"And you didn't think that was fucking relevant to tell me?"

I bite my lip, because Mount's tone sounds scarier than it has all night. The muscle in his jaw tenses when I don't answer.

"He held a gun on you and threatened to kill your family."

"Yes," I whisper.

"And scared you into agreeing to his plan?"

I nod sharply again before finding my voice. "If Scar says anything about me attacking him with a hammer and butcher knife when he burst in, you can tell him I thought he was Brett."

Mount's eyes widen, but his grip softens as his big thumb rubs back and forth along the skin of my arm. "Brett Hyde is never going to get the chance to do any of those things ever again."

I remember what Mount said about making me a widow, but outside the heat of self-defense, I'm not sure I'm cold-blooded enough to order his execution.

Instead, I say something that will allow me to sleep at night.

"You're right, because I'm going to give him what he wants. Then I'll never see him again."

Mount releases his hold on me. "I can't believe you'd consider giving him a dime."

I hold my hands out like scales. "Money or family?" I drop the one representing family and raise the one symbolizing money. "Family outweighs every dollar I could ever make. What's the point of any of it, if I don't have them?"

Mount's expression shutters. "You don't even speak to your sisters regularly."

I don't want to ask how he knows that, because I'm sure the answer will send me into another pacing rant. "That doesn't make them any less important to me. They're my blood. Wouldn't you sacrifice anything to save yours?"

Mount's dark eyes harden as he reaches into his pocket and pulls out his phone, his thumbs moving across the screen. When he returns it to its spot, he looks up at me.

"I have to go."

"Okay." I follow him toward the door, intent on leaving with him, but he stops at the doorway.

"Where do you think you're going?"

"Back to my gilded cage."

He shakes his head. "This is your new home. Get used to it. V will be stationed outside, so don't bother trying to leave."

"But—"

He shuts the door on my protest, trapping me in yet another luxurious prison.

As soon as Mount leaves, I yank open the door, because I've learned to be thorough.

Sure enough, just as he promised, Scar is stationed outside. Except, I guess his name is V. I prefer Scar, personally.

"My driver, and now my babysitter. How did you get so lucky?" Sarcasm drips from every word.

I slam the door in his face before he can respond, and rush to my purse when I hear my phone chime with a text alert. It's from the same unknown number that I now know belongs to Scar, and I save it in my phone as such.

> SCAR: *You want dinner? The chef will prepare something for you.*
> KEIRA: *I'm considering a hunger strike.*
> SCAR: *Boss won't like it.*
> KEIRA: *I don't give a NOLA-sized rat's ass about what he likes.*
> SCAR: *Then you're eating whatever I pick for you. Hope you like liver.*
> KEIRA: *Gross. You think he'll like you polluting his rooms with that stench?*
> SCAR: *Then pick something.*

I give it a moment of thought and come up with

the most ridiculous menu I can think of.

> KEIRA: *Turtle soup, New Zealand lobster tail, a grass-fed Argentinian filet, truffle mashed potatoes (the chunky kind but no skins), organic green beans amandine, and a chocolate soufflé with a side of fresh raspberry compote.*

With a triumphant smile, I wait for a return message and get nothing.

It doesn't dim my smugness. Now he can't blame me for not eating. I followed directions.

I wander the room, not wanting to pry, but unable to stop myself from peeking into the bedroom again and crossing the plush gold-and-black carpet to reach the palatial bathroom. The creamy white stone is shot through with veins of gold and black, and I can't help but wonder what his obsession is with those colors.

I shut down the curiosity because it's not going to help me get out of the situation I find myself in.

With my phone still in hand, I think of the one person who may be able to give me some kind of guidance.

I pull up Magnolia's last text and shoot her one back.

> KEIRA: *Need to talk ASAP. Shit is crazy.*

I wait several long moments, inspecting the gold fixtures on a bathtub the size of a small pool, and peer into the water closet that's larger than the entire bathroom in my apartment. There's even a freaking bidet. I'll admit I'm a little curious about how one uses that, because I've never tried.

My phone chimes and my attention cuts to the screen.

MAGNOLIA: *Got a business meeting tonight. How crazy?*
KEIRA: *Crazy enough that I think I'm losing my shit.*
MAGNOLIA: *I'll reschedule. Call ya in ten.*

I back out of the bathroom and kick off my heels once I reach the plush carpet, letting my feet sink into the thick pile.

Property in the French Quarter has ridiculous value per square foot. More than I could ever afford, and here Mount owns who knows how much. The curiosity I shoved down earlier returns, and I decide it's time to get as much information out of Magnolia as humanly possible about Lachlan Mount.

I owe him over two million dollars. The reality of the situation slaps me hard in the face.

How the hell am I going to repay him? Even if I pulled off an event like the one for the Voodoo Kings every month, and my sales quadrupled over the next two years, I'd still fall short. And that's not counting how much it would cost me to increase capacity to meet such an increase in demand.

Then again, Mount hasn't asked for a single payment in monetary terms, only in sexual favors.

My phone rings, and I realize I've lost track of time when Magnolia's number flashes across the screen. I answer immediately.

"Hey."

"What the hell is happening now?"

"Where do I even start?"

"The beginning, I'd suggest. Catch me up, Ke-ke."

So I do, starting with Brett's return from the dead.

"No. Fucking. Way. You have got to be shitting me. I was there, beneath that dark-as-shit veil, when you interred his ashes."

I insisted she didn't need it, but she didn't want to cause what she called *mama drama* at the service.

"Yeah, well, apparently those ashes weren't his, and someone bought off the medical examiner to say it was him."

"Doesn't take a genius to figure out who did that." She's not wrong. "Still doesn't explain who the hell was found in that car."

"I have no idea. I'm pretty sure I don't want to know."

"I bet Brett's wishing he'd stayed gone."

"Probably not, because he's going to walk away with more cash."

"You can't give it to him." Magnolia's reply is in the form of a pissy huff.

"I don't have a choice."

We talk about Brett for a few more minutes, and then she changes the subject because I can't be swayed from my path and the plan I've concocted with the duffel bag, trench coat, dark sunglasses, and dye packs.

Seems solid to me.

"So, what happened after Mount came to the rescue?"

"One, he didn't rescue me. He got there after Brett was gone, and his henchman got there first."

"Minor details, Ke-ke. Get to the good stuff."

Magnolia has always been bossy, and I brace myself for my next revelation.

"I found out that it was Mount the night of the masquerade. Not Brett."

"What. The. Fuck?" Magnolia's shock carries through her words. "How?"

I shake my head, even though she can't see me. "I don't know, but it's really freaking me out. That was the night I decided Brett was the one. The night I decided eloping with him was the best idea ever, because he was everything I wanted. But I was so freaking wrong. He wasn't even the guy."

"Jesus Christ, Ke-ke. Only you would get married because of one good fuck. Swear to God. And you didn't even marry the dick that gave it to you."

I throw my head back to stare at the glossy black ceiling. "It's not my fault! None of this makes any sense."

"And then what happened? There has to be more."

"We fought . . ." I pause, swallowing back the confession I'm still having trouble admitting. Strangely, this is even harder to get out than the part about the masquerade.

"And?" Magnolia prompts.

The only way I can get it out is to charge through

boldly, so that's exactly what I do. "He kissed me. He promised he wouldn't let my family get hurt, and then . . . well, you know."

"Back up for just one fucking second."

I can picture the hand gestures she's making right now as she processes the part I didn't want to admit.

"He *kissed* you?" Magnolia sounds more shocked about this than she did about my undead husband.

I decide to move the conversation along. "Yeah. And then—"

"No, stop. We gotta discuss this because . . . that's not Mount. He doesn't kiss any of the girls. I have to make damn sure they know it's a hard limit before I send them his way."

The implication of what she's saying slams into me. "Wait. Are you telling me *you* provide him with his mistresses? Are you freaking kidding me?"

"Ke-ke, you know what I do." Her tone sounds apologetic for a beat.

"But—"

"He wants girls from overseas, no locals. So I find them, vet them, ship them over, make sure they're properly trained in all his preferences and understand his rules, and then I turn them over to him. After that, I never see them again."

My heart slams into my ribs. "Why didn't you mention this before?"

"Because we don't talk about what I do. We pretend my profession doesn't exist when you're around. Besides, I told you everything I know. All the pertinent stuff, anyway."

"And the fact that you supply him with hookers wasn't pertinent?"

I'm yelling at Magnolia now, something I haven't done in years. Not since she got kicked out of school and I was pissed at her for losing her scholarship. At the same time, guilt flashes through me. She's right; we really don't talk about what she does. Ever. It's like the elephant in the room that I never want to mention. *Nice, Keira. Now you're the shitty friend.*

"They're not hookers. My girls are higher class than that, so watch that judgey tone you got going on."

Another wave of guilt follows, and I take a few deep breaths before I continue. "I'm sorry. I didn't mean that. But, please . . . you have to tell me everything you know because I'm currently standing in the man's bedroom, and clearly I don't know shit about him except for the little bits and pieces you've told me."

"Wait. You're in *his room?*" Magnolia stresses the last two words of the question like I might have misspoken.

"Yes. His room."

"What the hell? He's always kept his girls in a separate house. Easily accessible, but from what I heard, he never visited them anywhere else. Never took them out in public. Certainly never took them to his own damned room. This is a big fucking deal, Ke-ke. We need to search it."

I hold my phone out and stare down at the screen like her face will appear after that crazy suggestion. "What happened to you being worried this line was tapped?"

When I bring it back up to my ear, Magnolia's already rationalizing it. "What man would expect you *not* to go through his room when he leaves you there alone for the first time? This is practically standard procedure, so get to it. Now, move your ass. Let's start in the bathroom."

I drop onto the leather sectional. "I'm going to need more liquor before I have the balls to start digging through Mount's medicine cabinet."

"Then get you some damn liquor and get going. You don't have all night." In the background are rustling sounds, and then the clink of ice cubes in a glass. "I'm fixing myself a drink too, so we'll do it together, one room and one drink at a time."

I drop my forehead to my knees. "This might be your worst idea ever. After getting kicked out of school, obviously."

"Ke-ke, I've got everything I could possibly want, and it all started with that blow job in the school supply closet. Don't feel sorry for me. I made the best of a situation that could've ended up a whole lot worse."

Maybe she's right, but I still don't like thinking about it. *Annnd, there's some more guilt.*

"Get your bottle and your glass, because you can't tell me that man's room doesn't have any booze in it."

Again, Magnolia is always right.

"Fine. Hold on." I walk to the glass shelves holding all the liquor bottles, and survey them. "He doesn't have Seven Sinners in here."

"Well, good, because you won't get drunk enough to find your ladyballs with that anyway. Get a damn drink, Ke-ke. Hurry up."

"Fine." I grab a bottle of vodka from the top shelf. It's definitely a terrible plan, but since I can't stand Scotch or tequila, which seem to be my only other choices, this is the best I can do. I don't bother with a tumbler, just suck back a shot from the bottle itself.

"This shit is terrible," I say after I manage to choke it down. "How can people drink this?"

I read off the label of the bottle to her and she gets quiet.

"Most people will never get the chance, because that shit's like a thousand dollars a bottle."

Suddenly, the idea of draining it while I search for clues about the *real* Lachlan Mount doesn't seem quite so distasteful. "Okay, heading for the bathroom."

An hour later, I've searched the bathroom, the bedroom, and the living room—including every cabinet and drawer. I attempt and fail at picking the sole locked door with a hairpin.

"This is hopeless. I should've watched more YouTube videos."

"Then do it now and call me back."

I flop back onto the most comfortable bed my body has ever touched. "I can't. It's all spinning, Mags."

"Shit. You're such a lightweight when it comes to anything but whiskey. Makes no damn sense."

"When does the spinning stop?"

"After you either throw up or pass out."

"Ewww. I don't want to puke."

"Good, because you're no rookie, so don't act like it. You laying down?"

"Yeah."

"Then hang your leg over the side so you can touch the floor. That should help with the spinnin'."

"Okay."

"You put everything back where you found it, right?"

"Mm-hmm, yeah. Ten-four, Magpie."

"Shit. You're really drunk."

"True story." I yawn. "Gotta go. The spinny thing is gettin' worse. I'll try the leg trick. I'm tired."

"Yeah, and from the way you're slurring, you're gonna hate yourself in the morning."

"That's a given, 'cause I gotta give that piece of shit Brett all the money Mount put in my account so I don't go bankrupt. Fucker." At this point, I don't know who I'm talking about.

"I don't think Mount's gonna let that happen, Ke-ke."

"He can't stop me."

"Okay, sweetheart. You get some sleep now. Set your alarm."

"Already did. Night, Mags. Love you."

"Love you too. And before you pass out, you need to get it through your head that nothing about how Mount is treating you is normal. If I had to guess, I'd say you're making him break all the rules."

"Mount makes all the damn rules. None of them apply to him."

I disconnect the call before she can respond. Or I

try, but the phone lands on my face, cracking me in the nose.

"Ugh. Fucking Russians. Who could possibly like that shit more than whiskey?"

It's the last thought I remember before I fall asleep.

NINE

Mount

FROM MY POSITION ON THE DOCK, I stare down at the fucking idiot bound hand and foot in the bottom of Ransom's airboat. Saxon stands beside him, and we all wait for the douchebag to wake up so he has a few minutes to realize just how badly he fucked up by breaking his end of the bargain and coming back to life.

Saxon shoves the toe of a muddy boot into the man's ribs. Brett Hyde's head jerks back, his lids flickering open but closing again as the spotlight Ransom holds shines directly into his eyes.

"Bet you wishin' you stayed dead, Brett," Ransom says, his tone conversational and his bayou accent as strong as ever.

"What the hell happened?" Brett's words slur, probably because I didn't spare any force when I pistol-whipped him into unconsciousness.

Ransom nudges him. "Givin' you a chance to send

a prayer up to the Almighty before we take you out for one last midnight ride."

Ransom's a silver-tongued bayou rat who started smuggling around the time I was adopted into the empire I now rule. There's not a corner of these swamps he doesn't know, and luckily for me, he doesn't give a shit about what he's transporting as long as the price is right.

I don't have friends, but if I did, I might consider him one. We've done plenty of business over the last twenty years.

Out of the two of them, he's the talker. I suppose it helps in the transport business.

Saxon prefers to stick to the shadows and speak as little as possible. But I've never met a man better with a gun, knife, garrote, or even a fucking pencil when it comes to killing. He's a true professional in every sense of the word, and I trust him with my most sensitive jobs. I wouldn't even let my own employees touch the shit I have him handle. I've never met a man who has his emotions locked down tighter than Saxon. *Smart motherfucker.*

Instead of sending up a prayer, Brett Hyde takes the chance to run his mouth.

"Fuck y'all. Fuck that cunt bitch too. Spoiled little princess. Is she taking it up the ass from you to get your help saving her precious distillery? Is she so good you're payin' her for it? Maybe I shoulda spent more time in that pussy." Blood bubbles from between Brett's missing teeth when he talks, and I feel no remorse when Saxon lands another kick to his face, cracking a few more.

"Shut your fucking mouth, you piece of shit."

Brett spits out his broken teeth. "You're the piece of shit, Mount. I heard you were found covered in it."

It occurs to me in that moment, I couldn't give a shit if he insults me. He's down to the final minutes of his life. But even so, insults against Keira will be met with more and more pain.

"You held a gun on your fucking wife and threatened to kill her family. I'd say you're winning the piece-of-shit contest," Ransom says.

Brett glares at him. "I didn't marry her for that cunt she's got. I wanted the money. Thought she was the cash cow, ticket to easy street. But she had that fucking distillery in debt up to its eyeballs as soon as she took over. I could only skim a few dollars here and there because she had hardly any extra left." He coughs up more blood before continuing. "And fuck her family too."

Saxon kicks him in the ribs once more, and Ransom goes off again.

"Don't you know it's disrespectful to talk about your fucking wife that way? For fuck's sake, what the hell is wrong with you? You took vows."

Hyde spits blood on the deck of the boat. "Fuck, it wasn't real. I married some bitch in Reno when I was twenty-five and never got that shit taken care of. Keira was never really my wife. Total waste as a fuck and a mark."

I jump off the dock and land in the bottom of the boat on both feet, rocking it from side to side. "You were already married? Are you fucking kidding me?"

Hyde nods. "What do you care? If you thought you

72

were gonna find a gold mine in that distillery, joke's on you because they ain't never gonna make a dollar. Screwed yourself on that deal, Mount."

I crouch down and speak low, so only Brett can hear. "That's where you're wrong, you worthless piece of shit. I got everything I wanted out of this deal. It was never about the money. It was always about *her*."

Brett's eyes go wide in the spotlight as realization sets in. "No fucking—"

I stand up and land a kick to his face, wishing I could finish this job myself, but I won't. There's somewhere else I'd rather be.

I climb out of the boat and look at Saxon. "Get creative. Take your time with it too. He doesn't need to die fast."

"Hey—" Brett protests, but Saxon kicks him in the head and he goes silent again.

Saxon turns back in my direction and gives me a nod.

Knowing that piece of shit was never actually married to Keira doesn't change anything, but it will surely matter to her. Then again, it just shows how badly she was conned.

Maybe I won't tell her. It won't matter in a few minutes anyway.

I step out of the boat and look at Saxon. "You got this?"

He almost looks insulted at my question. "Of course."

My gaze shifts to Ransom. "Make sure the body's never found."

Ransom laughs. "After all these years, you think I need directions like that? Besides, I got a couple hungry gators waitin' to be fed."

I reach for my phone and open a secure app. With a few taps, my part is completed. "Your money's already in your accounts. I want to know when it's done."

"Yes, sir," Ransom says, and Saxon just nods.

Saxon gags Brett as Ransom fires up the deafening engine of the airboat.

I turn on the dock and head toward the nondescript black Mercedes I drove out to the meet when I got the notification from Saxon that he had the package and Ransom was ready to dispose of it.

The airboat flies away from the dock, skidding across the water around a turn, disappearing out of sight before I start the car.

As I drive back toward the Quarter, I can't help but think about how fucked up this day has been on every level. Brett. Keira freaking out. Her attacking me, and somehow setting off an impulse I've never had in my entire life.

I kissed her.

I've never kissed a woman, just like I've never fucked another woman without a condom. Ever. Keira Kilgore is the exception.

It pisses me off to know that Brett Hyde was never the barrier I thought, and yet I let him stand in the way. *He was already married.*

Why the hell didn't my people find that marriage certificate in his records? My PI has a fuck-ton of explaining to do.

I'm still shaking my head at how big of a dumb fuck Brett Hyde was. If he was even minutely less stupid than I thought, he'd have made sure that shit was legal so he'd be guaranteed a piece of the assets. The more important point? *Keira was legally free the whole time.*

I could have swept in and taken over so much sooner. Then again, Keira needed to realize what a piece of shit Hyde was all by herself. When I caught word that she'd secured her own place and was meeting with a divorce lawyer, I knew it was my turn. *Finally.* It still pisses me off to think about the time I wasted.

But now, she's really fair game. There's not a goddamned thing stopping me from keeping her indefinitely.

The devil that always rides on my shoulder chimes in with his opinion. *Or you could get rid of her right the fuck now because she's making you weak.*

I'd like to say there's an angel offering an opposite perspective on the other side, but there never has been and never will be.

I don't reach my suite until hours later. Because of that fucking voice, I forced myself to make my normal rounds on the gaming-room floor to see and be seen. I won't deviate from my pattern, because I refuse to acknowledge that the voice could be right.

Once I'm satisfied, I head through the passageways and push open the door that leads into my living area. The first thing that hits me is the strange aroma of food coming from the coffee table. I lift the silver covers to find soup, lobster, steak, and God knows what else. All of it untouched.

The nightstand lamp on the bedside table is still on, and Keira is passed out on top of the covers fully clothed, clutching what looks to be my most expensive bottle of vodka. An *empty* bottle of vodka, to be more accurate.

Her phone is next to her head, and I reach over to pick it up, expecting the movement to wake her. It doesn't. When her mouth opens and she releases a soft snore, I know there's not a chance in hell she'll be rising before noon, which suits me just fine.

Carefully, I remove the vodka bottle and roll her to her side to unzip her skirt and remove it, along with her blouse. The lingerie beneath is sexy as hell, but the curves of her body are what make my dick harden against the silk lining of my pants.

Not tonight, I think, willing my body to calm the hell down. *She's mine, which means tomorrow I'll get what I want.*

I remove the bra because I can't imagine that would be comfortable to sleep in, and can't help but admire the pale skin of her tits and those perfect pink nipples that pucker in the cool air of the room.

Not tonight, I remind myself, and tuck her under the covers naked, like that will somehow dull the temptation she presents.

Like Eve in that fucking garden. Adam never stood a chance.

A rush of satisfaction fills me to see her wild red mane spread out on my black satin pillowcase like fire. I've never had a woman in this bed before, but I'd be lying if I said I hadn't pictured this exact moment more times than I'll ever admit.

I knew I wanted Keira Kilgore in my bed, but what I didn't see coming was how much she'd challenge me outside of it—and how addictive gaining her submission would become.

I back away from the bed slowly and retreat to my closet to shed my suit. I make a mental note that I need to contact G tomorrow to arrange for a full wardrobe for Keira. Up until now, I've had him provide only specific outfits at my request, but things have changed.

When I slide under the covers beside her, she moans and curls her body toward me as she shivers. If she were conscious, she'd never do that, so I take advantage and pull her back against my front. My body heat soaks into her skin, and I wrap an arm around her waist.

She makes a noise, like her brain is fighting to regain consciousness.

"Sleep," I whisper, and in moments, she releases another soft snore. The fact that I think it's cute tells me just how fucked I am.

I told Hyde the truth; it was never about the money. It was always about her. He was too blind to see a treasure when he had it in his hands, but I'm not.

I see Keira Kilgore exactly for what she's

becoming—the one woman who might be strong enough to stand by my side and rule an empire.

She'd stare at me in horror if I told her that right now. She needs discipline first, and what's more, she *wants* it. I've never met a more stubborn woman with such a strong submissive streak. I look forward to taming it but don't want to extinguish her fire, only guide it in a different direction. Tomorrow is soon enough to explain the rules of how things are going to work going forward.

She snuggles into me in her sleep, and I wonder what it would take to make her this pliant while awake. Short of drugs or alcohol, that is.

I close my eyes, not anticipating getting a single moment of sleep with my brain moving a million miles an hour, but shockingly, I drift off in minutes with Keira's body pressed against mine.

TEN

Keira

AN UNFAMILIAR CHIME FROM MY PHONE WAKES ME out of a nightmare. My hands are bound behind my back and I'm on my knees, begging a faceless man to kill me.

With chills racing across my skin, I jerk up in bed, the tides of fear from the dream receding until my eyes snap open and I find myself in a dark room. I reach for my phone as the chime rings again, and use the glowing screen to illuminate the room as my head throbs.

Mount's room.

Last night.

The vodka.

"Oh fuck!" I jump out of bed, remembering what I have to do today.

My appointment is at ten a.m. at the bank. I'm supposed to withdraw the cash, put it in a duffel bag, and then walk outside and around the block and drop the duffel bag through the open back window of the black Suburban that will be parked at the curb.

I've run through the plan so many times in my head, I'm ready to rock.

A cool breeze sweeps through the room, and my nipples pucker. I cover them with my hands, shocked when I touch skin.

What the hell? I didn't fall asleep naked.

That means . . . I search the dark room for the man who must have stripped me last night, but there's no noise coming from anywhere in the room.

Using the glow of my phone, I stumble to the door to flip the switch of the overhead lights. I am most definitely naked.

That bastard.

My gaze drops to the time on the phone screen, and I convince myself I'm still drunk when I see the appointment reminder . . . for *noon* . . . in fifteen minutes. *Is that why the chime that woke me sounded different?*

I blink twice, because there's no way in hell I'm really seeing that time. I set two alarms so I wouldn't miss my rendezvous with my not-so-dead husband. There's no way I slept through both of them. Is there?

I tap on the appointment reminder, and the full text pops up.

Your prior appointment has been handled. Your creditor, however, requires your presence in the private study at noon because you've got debts to pay and they're past due.

Open the nightstand drawer. Wear what's inside.
Bring the leather box to me through the door you
attempted to open last night.
Do not speak until you're spoken to.

The last line makes my palm itch to slap him, but I'm quickly distracted by the rest of the cryptic message.

What the hell does *your prior appointment has been handled* mean? Does that mean he paid off Brett? Or . . .

I don't want to consider the alternative, because the only thing that matters right now is my family's safety. I tap the phone icon and pull up my mom's cell phone number. It rings three times, and I pace the room as I wait for her to answer.

She doesn't. And her cheery voice-mail message is no comfort.

"Sorry I missed you! I'm probably on the golf course right now. Text me, and I'll call you back when I finish on the eighteenth green."

My dad's cell phone is next. It rings twice before he picks up, and I heave a sigh of relief.

"Oh, thank God."

"What's wrong? Did something happen at the distillery?"

In that moment, my dad's gruff voice is the best sound I've ever heard. I don't even care that retirement hasn't changed him and the distillery always comes first.

"No, no problem. I just wanted to make sure you

and Mom were okay. Is everything fine?"

"You having one of those walking-over-your-grave moments? Is that what this is?" my dad asks, always the superstitious one.

I swallow back the fear that gathered in my belly when I got my mom's voice-mail recording. "You could say that. When Mom didn't pick up, I worried."

"We're fine. She's out with Jury getting their nails done. For some reason or another, she decided to show up at our door last night with nothing but a backpack. I swear to God, that girl will never grow up. She's too old to be acting like this still."

"Jury's there? Did she say why?" I'm actually happy to hear it. That's one less member of my family I have to make sure is breathing this morning after I didn't follow through on my end of the bargain with Brett.

Little by little, the rigidity of my spine eases.

"She said she's between jobs. Needs a place to crash, and figured she might as well see us and kill two birds with one stone. I swear, if she starts dancing on bars around here, I'll never live it down at the club."

I close my eyes, thankful to hear my father bitching about my sister like he usually does, instead of the horrible alternative.

"I'm sure she won't, Dad. Have you talked to Imogen lately?"

He grunts. "She's too busy for any of us. Got a text from her this morning that she applied for some fancy postdoctoral program, and she needs letters of reference from people who aren't family. But she doesn't want my help to get them. Just suggestions on who to ask."

That also sounds *exactly* like my middle sister. She's determined to do everything herself, even if it means making things ten times harder. It's like she's afraid asking for help will make her accomplishments somehow mean less.

Sound a little familiar? an inner voice taunts. I tell it to shut up.

"So, everything's good? Your golf game is improving?"

"Yeah, yeah. I'm bored as hell. I'm running the condo association, but I'm thinking of taking on a couple consulting jobs to keep me busy. I can only play so much damn golf. Your mom drags me out every friggin' day."

"Dad—"

"Don't you dare tell your mother about that. We've already had it out. I'm not meant to be retired, though. It's the dumbest thing I've ever done."

"Maybe just try relaxing?"

He huffs. "You do any of that lately?"

I can't even begin to tell him what my life has been like, so I give him the win on that point. "Touché."

"I worked hard and played hard, girl. Don't wait until you're my age to have fun. Probably should go find yourself a real man before you're too old."

"Dad!"

"What? We both know I'm right. That bastard didn't deserve you. Too slick. Don't let the next one fool ya, girl. Make sure you got his number from the very beginning."

I smile weakly, even though he can't see me. "Sure, Dad. But it'll be a *long, long* time before that happens."

"You never know. We're Irish. We believe in fate. The right man will find you, and he won't let you go when he recognizes what he's got."

That's probably the biggest compliment my father has ever bestowed upon me, besides having the confidence to sell me the distillery and let his retirement depend on me running it.

Tears gather in the corners of my eyes. "Thanks, Dad. I love you."

"Love you too, Keir. Call me if you want to hire me for a consulting gig. I know a thing or two about whiskey."

"You'd be my first call."

We hang up, and the warmth of my father's compliment evaporates when my phone chimes as another reminder pops up on the screen.

You have ten minutes to follow my instructions or pay the consequences.

"Shit!"

I don't want to know what Mount has planned for today, but I do know one thing—I need answers. What does his note on the first appointment reminder mean? I need to know.

I toss the phone on the bed, glaring at it and wondering how he hacked into my calendar, but that's not the problem I need to focus on right now.

Staring at the black lacquered nightstand, I take

two measured steps before pulling open the top drawer. Inside is a box from an expensive lingerie store I could never imagine shopping at. I lift it out, open the lid, and peel back thin tissue to reveal a bustier, a garter belt, and thigh-high stockings so thin, they have to be silk.

I search the box for the remaining item of clothing that I assume must also be inside, but there's no thong or panties. I look in the drawer, and the only other item inside is a black leather box.

Those never contain anything good, I scoff, but apparently my inner voice decides to play devil's advocate. *Except for when they lead to orgasms.*

Do I want to open it? I consider the question for all of half a second before I flip the lid.

What. The. Fuck.

Nestled in black velvet is a ball gag and a silver butt plug, this one wider than the last.

If he expects me to—

My phone chimes again from the bed with another appointment reminder.

> *Five-minute warning. Your shoes will be*
> *waiting outside the door.*

That arrogant asshole. I'm not waiting five minutes. He has a hell of a lot of explaining to do.

With the leather box clutched in my hand, I take a step toward the door whose lock I drunkenly tried to pick with hairpins last night. I freeze before I make it a second step.

Do I wear the lingerie and obey?

I look down at my naked form and haul in a deep breath. There's no way in hell I'm walking in there like this.

I reach for the lingerie, pausing when I realize I can smell the booze seeping out of my pores.

Yuck. Even I'm not willing to defile those beautiful clothes by putting them on without rinsing off first. Plus . . . maybe if I appear sweet and obedient, I'll get the answers I want faster than if I flip Mount the bird and defy his orders.

The clock on my phone shows I've wasted another minute deliberating, which means I have exactly four minutes to rinse off and get changed.

Screw it. I rush to the bathroom and grab a toothbrush and toothpaste off the counter before stepping into the massive shower and turning the spray to hot. I brush my teeth, not caring that it's Mount's toothbrush, as I scrub last night off my body.

Conscious of the seconds ticking away on my deadline, I practically scald myself flipping the tap off, then snag a fluffy towel to wrap around me.

I toss my borrowed items back on the counter and dry off as fast as I can before shimmying into the bustier and tying its silk ribbon in a bow. I take extra care with the stockings, not wanting to snag them as I slide each one up a leg. Finally, I step into the garter belt and hook the clips to the top of the stockings.

A final chime sounds on my phone, and I want to hurl the thing at the wall. Instead, I read the latest appointment reminder.

You're late. For every minute that passes,
I'm taking it out on your ass.

A shiver rushes through me, hardening my nipples, even though I tell myself that doesn't mean anything good. I saw the butt plug. So, what the hell does *taking it out on your ass* mean?

I rush to the door, almost tripping on a pair of sky-high black pumps that can't be called anything but what they are—hooker heels. But in this case, they're the really expensive kind.

I don't think before sliding my feet inside. I touch the door handle, but immediately remember the last thing I'm missing and scramble back to the bed to grab the leather box.

My phone reads 12:05. I really am late.

Hell. This isn't going to be good.

I hurry to the door again, steadying myself as I twist the knob and push it open.

The room I'd tried to break into the night before isn't like the infamous *red room of pain* like I'd imagined, but an office. For some crazy reason, I actually feel a little let down. I thought for sure Mount would have some kinky room in this place, but apparently he's not quite the sexual deviant I thought he was.

Or I just haven't found it yet.

From behind the wide desk, much like in his other office, he fixes his dark eyes on my body as I step inside the room and close the door behind me. Voices come from his phone, which he has on speaker, and I realize he must be on a conference call.

He crooks a finger in my direction as he speaks. "Now that we have everyone necessary present, let's begin. Yakamora, you can start."

Yakamora, a name that's unfamiliar to me, begins discussing market fluctuations and hedges against risk. I can't tell if Mount is paying any attention to him because his gaze never leaves mine as I walk toward him on my towering heels, the leather box in hand.

"I understand your aversion to risks, but none of us would be where we are if we hadn't taken them," Mount says. "Casso, you want to share your opinion?"

A deep voice with an Italian accent fills the room next, but I'm not paying attention to his words because I've stopped a foot away from Mount. His dark gaze starts at the toes of my fuck-me heels and drags up the sheer black stockings, pausing on my pierced hood for a moment before rising to the garter belt and then the bustier.

"Just because those methods have worked for the old guard doesn't mean they're going to continue to work. If we want to maintain any control over what's happening, we have to be united in our approach," Mount says as his gaze finally reaches my face.

When the man with the Japanese accent begins to argue, Mount holds out a hand to me, palm up.

What does he want? I only wonder for a moment before I realize he's waiting for the box clenched in my grip. I offer it to him, partly terrified and partly thrilled at the thought of him using either or both of the items it contains on me.

What the hell is wrong with me? I shouldn't want this.

But I do.

Now that I know he's on a conference call, the gag makes sense, but it doesn't make it any less intimidating. Mount sets the box on his desk as the call continues, a roundtable of opinions, and from little bits and pieces I'm comprehending, it has to do with nothing I want to know about.

Mount lifts the gag out first, his dark gaze almost seeming to spark. He reaches his right hand out to hit the mute button on the speaker. "You ever wear one of these before?"

I shake my head, unintentionally following his order not to speak, but I literally have nothing to say.

His smile takes on that predatory quality I'm beginning to recognize means he's pleased and aroused. "Good."

He unmutes the phone first before standing and pressing the gag against my lips, as if daring me to speak.

In our skirmishes, I'm rarely obedient, but I'm not sure I want to find out what the punishment would be for interrupting this conference call with my protests. Besides, the rationalization fits right into my dark fascination with the device.

With the ball in my mouth, he fastens the strap behind my head. Now that my ability to speak freely is gone, my other senses are heightened and my nipples harden under the thin cups of the bustier. Mount reaches out and flicks one with a thumb. A muffled whimper escapes my lips as I squeeze my legs together, my new jewelry already causing wetness to gather between my thighs.

Mount mouths something at me, and it takes me a second to realize what he's saying.

Bad girl.

He grasps me by the hips before turning me around and pressing one hand to the small of my back until I'm bent over his desk directly in the middle. Mount retakes his seat and replies to a question on the call, but I'm too lost in the thought of how obscene I must look from behind, my pussy and ass exposed and right in his face.

My thighs clench together again. I want to stop myself from getting wetter, but it doesn't matter what this man does to me. My body falls prey to him every time.

I flinch when his hand moves, but relax when his palm smooths down my skin, caressing my ass. He strokes with his thumb and skims beneath the curve of my cheek. Then he changes direction, his finger skating up the edge of my crack, and my nerve endings jump to attention.

His touch disappears for a moment, and I open my eyes to see him pressing the mute button again.

Before I can make a sound, his palm connects with my right cheek with a slap. This time, there's no adjusting to the heat before it connects again and again, not stopping until both cheeks are burning with five smacks.

One for each minute I was late. I squeeze my eyes shut as he unmutes the phone and resumes lazily stroking my burning ass while he carries on with the conference call, never missing a beat.

Somehow, some way, the punishment only makes me wetter. I attempt to force my mind away from the sensations rampaging through me and onto the conversation, but it's a useless endeavor. My eyes drift closed as I sink into a state of heightened sensitivity, my mind focused only on Mount's touch. It's almost soothing, this lazy stroking of my body and the sound of his voice as he leads the call with authority.

At least, until his thumb slides between my legs and skims through the moisture gathered there.

The gag quiets my moan, but the person speaking at that moment pauses.

"Did someone have an objection?"

Mount is quick to reply. "Just my secretary. She's been very inefficient this morning at following directions."

All the men on the call laugh. They're probably all arrogant assholes like the one currently teasing me with my own wetness by dragging his index finger back and forth through it.

"Just bend her over the desk and show her who's boss. That's what I did in the old days."

It's the Italian man who comments, and while I'd like to punch him in the face, I'm too busy holding in another moan.

Mount's teasing torture lasts for so long that I completely lose track of time. The call continues as he pushes two fingers inside me, stretching and slowly fin-ger-fucking me until I'm squirming against the desk. In that moment, I'm thankful for the gag because I want to beg him for more. Instead, I grip the opposite edge of the wood, attempting to stay silent and repress my reactions.

Mount is skilled in his torture, however, and when he draws the moisture back to circle my tightest hole, I begin to unravel.

I'm still not used to it. I don't think I'll ever be totally used to it, but my nerve endings fire pleasure signals to my brain and I push back against his touch instinctively. This time, Mount's hand reaches out to tap the mute button before applying more pressure.

"I finger-fucked your pussy, and now it's time for your ass. You think you can keep quiet?"

I don't respond. Obviously, because my powers of speech are impeded by the gag, but also because I want to curse him for stealing all control over my body from me.

While I focus on staying still, Mount opens a drawer and pulls out something I can't see. As soon as cool liquid dribbles down my crack, I recognize it as lube. He gathers it up, coating his finger, and uses it to tease me.

"Press back. Help me push inside. Show me you want it."

Mount pushes forward and my hips slide back on instinct, helping him press against the tight ring of muscle and tearing another moan from my lips.

Luckily, the call is still on mute.

"I'm going to fuck your ass with my finger while I talk to some of the most powerful men in the world, and then I'm going to fuck you with that plug and tease your clit with that new piercing until you're dying to come, but you won't. You know why?"

I shake my head, wishing I could curse him.

"Because it's about time you work a little harder on chipping away at the balance of that debt, and I get to come first."

His arrogant words don't anger me. Instead, they make me even more determined to steal as much pleasure as I can for myself, no matter what he does to me.

Why should he be the only one enjoying this? Besides, I can't deny that I'm beyond turned on by being facedown on his desk while he takes advantage of me.

How many nights have I worked in my office, wishing the dominant man of my dreams would come in, shove all the papers aside, and bend me over before doing whatever he wants to me?

More than I'll ever admit.

This may be Mount's game, but it's my fantasy come to life.

When he pushes forward with his fingertip again, I shock both of us by pressing my hips back against him until he breaches the muscle. When he pulls back, I rub my piercing on the edge of the desk, stealing pleasure from anywhere I can get it.

"Don't you dare come," Mount says before he pushes his finger firmly into my ass, fucking me slowly over and over again, and then unmutes the phone.

Don't come? That's one order I have no intention of following.

I'm *so close*, between my hypersensitive clit and his finger in my ass when he pulls free.

I jerk my head around so I can look back at him.

"I think we need to reevaluate our assets and decide what we can afford to redeploy to get a true assessment of their resources," Mount says, using his free hand to reach for the plug. "We can't conquer them until we understand exactly how much power they have at their disposal."

Even though the words are directed to the men on the other end of the call, Mount's words echo through my head. *We can't conquer them until we understand exactly how much power they have.*

In that moment, I make a promise to myself, one I swear I won't break this time. *Mount will never know how much power he has over me.* If he were ever to learn, I have no doubt he'd exploit it even more than he is now as he presses the tip of the plug to my ass.

The cold metal sends me lifting off the desk with a harsh indrawn breath, but Mount covers the sound with the rustling of some papers.

"Are we in agreement on this point, gentlemen?"

The others agree as Mount pushes the plug the rest of the way inside, until the flared base is seated against the outside rim of my hole.

"Good, because I think we're about ready to move on to our next topic for discussion. Casso, you brought up the next issue on the agenda, so why don't you fill the rest of us in."

Mount rises from his seat and reaches into the drawer for some kind of antibacterial wipes and cleans the finger he just pushed into my ass.

The metal inside me is warming to body temperature, but it's unyielding, much like the man who inserted it.

As soon as he's cleaned up, Mount responds to the conversation and the dialogue continues. At this point, I'm clueless as to what's being discussed. They could literally be talking about cloning unicorns, and I wouldn't know. Mount's hands grip my hips, and he flips me over onto my back before hitting MUTE again.

"Before this call is over, I'm fucking either your mouth or ass. I'm feeling benevolent today, so even though you were *late*, I'll let you decide." He glances at the time on the phone. "You've got about five minutes to make your decision."

Mouth or ass?

As I contemplate the choices, Mount leans down and circles my clit with his tongue, flicking the piercing. He hasn't unmuted the call, so I buck upward at him, trying to fuck his face all the way to orgasm. Mount lifts his head and delivers a stinging smack to my pussy, just missing my new jewelry.

"My naughty secretary is trying to fuck my face and come before I get mine." His eyes narrow on mine. "That's the one thing I won't let you get away with today. I'm taking a sweet piece of what belongs to me."

He fucks my pussy with his tongue until someone directs a question to him and he unmutes the call again. "That's acceptable. We can make that work."

It's clear the call is winding down, which means that so is my time to choose. I swore before that I wouldn't kiss him, and he destroyed that boundary. I told him I wouldn't go to my knees for him either, but considering the alternative and the fact that his cock is thicker than this plug, I know what choice I have to make.

Mount is breaking my rules one at a time, and with each one, I lose a part of the woman I've always been, but gain a piece of the woman I never knew I could be.

I finally understand the reason it's called power exchange, but with Mount and me, it's more accurately termed a power struggle.

He takes. I fight.

He threatens. I rebel.

He taunts. I argue.

It's a never-ending cycle, and at this point, with his tongue teasing my entrance, I'm not sure I care to continue it today.

Instead, I bury my fingers in his hair and press upward, but one universal truth continues—Mount is stronger than me. He lifts his head, a wicked grin on his face as he plunges two fingers inside me.

"Agreed," says the Japanese man.

"Agreed." The Italian concurs.

"Agreed," Mount says, but I have to wonder if he has any clue what he just committed to. "If that's all, gentlemen, I've got another matter to attend to, and will follow up with any additional thoughts via email."

Good-byes are exchanged, and Mount finally hangs up. He pulls his fingers from my pussy and sucks them clean.

"Which is it? Ass or mouth?"

I lift my chin, reminding him there's no way I can reply.

"You can point. If I'm fucking your ass, then there's no need to remove the gag." A hint of a smile tugs at the corner of his mouth.

Smug asshole. He gains a ridiculous amount of enjoyment from taunting me. Mount expects me to rebel, even anticipates it. *I'm beginning to recognize his tells, so that's something.*

I lift my hand. Using my middle finger, I point to the ball gag lodged in my mouth.

His expression flares with heat. "Fucking finally."

His phone rings again, and he looks at the receiver.

"And you're just in time for my next call." His gaze pins mine. "Get on your knees."

Again with the power struggle, but this time, I decide to throw him off track, since he thinks he knows exactly what to expect from me.

Not today.

Today, I'm going to show Mount what it's like to have his iron-clad control over his body stolen from him.

I hope he doesn't have any plans to pay attention to this next call, because he's not going to remember a goddamned thing.

ELEVEN

Mount

HER RED HAIR DOESN'T EVEN BEGIN TO DO JUSTICE to her temper. Keira Kilgore has a fierce fighting spirit, the likes of which I've never seen in a woman.

Her little middle-finger salute will earn her a punishment—her least favorite kind, I'm coming to realize. *No orgasm.* Then she'll curse me, and I'll have another reason to bend her over my lap and spank the round ass currently filled with a plug that's still smaller than my dick, but we're getting her stretched out.

Soon.

But first, I'm going to get something I've been waiting for since that very first night.

I lower myself back into my chair and nod at the floor between my spread legs. The flare of rebellion in her green gaze tells me that she has plans for me.

It's exactly the test I need to prove to myself that no matter what happens, she doesn't have the power to distract me from my business.

She is not a weakness, I vow as she hits her knees. I already feel triumph flowing in my veins as I unbuckle the gag from around the back of her head.

She stretches her jaw one way and then the other, no doubt stiff from wearing a gag for the first time, but I swear it won't be the last. I don't always need Keira mouthing off to tell me what she thinks of me; I can read it in her every expression. She has no shield. No mask. Everything is transparent on her face.

Right now, she's thinking she can destroy my concentration and steal my control.

Never going to happen, hellion.

She does surprise me when she doesn't attempt to speak. Maybe it's the Spanish-accented words coming through the phone that I continue to answer with rote responses, or maybe it's because she's just that intent on her task. Either way, my quads tense when she flips open the button on my slacks, slides down the zipper, and my dick bobs free. Her red hair spills forward around her face, hiding my cock and her mouth from view.

Fuck that.

I'm going to watch as she takes every inch of me down her throat, even if I have to stand and guide it myself, teaching her the tricks to tame her gag reflex.

I bury my hands in her hair, pulling it away from her face as I help guide her movements. She laves the head of my dick with her tongue, and her unpracticed technique fills me with that same conqueror mentality I had when she admitted she'd never tried anal play.

How does it feel to be corrupted, Keira? I don't ask

the question aloud, instead asking it with my eyes, but she misses the taunt because her full attention is on my cock. I'm not about to complain about that.

What she lacks in skill, she makes up for with enthusiasm as she attempts to take me deep for the first time. She doesn't come close to taking all of me. She tongues my cock as she retreats, and then jacks me off with her hand when she has to take a breath.

Fuck me if her clear inexperience doesn't make me harder and push me to come faster than the most skilled mistress I've ever had.

My attention drifts away from the call as she tries to take me deeper each time, but gags before she swallows another inch.

Fuck.

Call be damned.

One of the men on the other end of the call asks me a question, and I reach out and slap a button to hang up.

The Mexicans will be pissed, but I don't give a shit. Right now, all I care about is feeding my thick cock down my little Irish hellion's throat.

Her head jerks up when I end the call, the head of my dick leaving her mouth with a pop, but I shake my head.

"You're not even close to finished, not until you take it all the way."

Her jaw drops, her mouth wide, no doubt ready to protest, but I take advantage by wrapping one hand around her face and holding her mouth open with my thumb.

"Every single fucking inch of my cock is going down your throat before you leave this room. You understand me?"

Her eyes flash with defiance that just makes my dick harder. I lay my other hand on her cheek, cupping her jaw with both palms.

"I'm gonna fuck your face, and you're going to take it like the dirty girl we both know you are. If you say one word to argue with me, I'll flip you over on this desk, take that plug out, and finish in your tight little ass."

Instead of fear, which would have been an understandable reaction, her pupils dilate and she squeezes her thighs together, dropping a hand from my knee to reach between them.

"Touch that pussy, and I'll clamp your clit beneath your piercing and make you scream for mercy while I deny you orgasm after orgasm." My threat freezes her movements, and I continue. "Put your hand back on my knee."

Defiance flares again in her expression but she complies, and her obedience spurs me on.

"Have you ever had your face properly fucked?"

She swallows, and shakes her head.

I tuck my thumbs into both corners of her mouth, forcing her jaw open. "Good. Because I'm about to teach you, and later, there will definitely be a test."

When I open her mouth, she sweeps her tongue across her lips, wetting the tips of my thumbs in the process.

"That's right, make sure those dick-sucking lips are

slick, because your lesson is about to start."

I rise, my hands still guiding her jaw open, but I angle my dick down as I push it into the hot, wet heaven of her mouth. Keira groans on my cock, and the vibrations carry straight through to my balls.

When my phone rings again, I rip the cord out of it.

No more interruptions.

Fuck the rest of the world, because I'm going to come down Keira Kilgore's throat.

For months, I've tortured myself with thoughts of her being touched by another man, knowing that eventually, I'd have her at my mercy. Now the time has come, I'm glad she's untrained. It means that douchebag Hyde didn't tend to her properly, which is why every single one of my encounters with her has been so explosive.

Keira needs a real man to show her what she's been missing out on, and I'm here to handle the job . . . and her.

TWELVE

Keira

OH SHIT. I KNOW I'M OUT OF MY LEAGUE WHEN HE stands and begins to push his cock in and out of my mouth with measured strokes, each one going deeper until I'm gagging on his dick.

His thumbs stroke my face and my jaw. "Easy. Breathe through your nose. You can take me. You *will* fucking take all of me."

His orders and commands don't fuel my rebellion at this moment. No, I'm too busy feeling the victory from the way he ended his call and returned one hundred percent of his attention to me.

Mount is fucking with my life, but I'm fucking with his too. And then he rips the cord out of the phone? Priceless.

The head of his cock hits the back of my throat again before I'm ready for it, and I gag once more.

Mount shakes his head. "Next time, swallow me down when you feel the urge to gag."

He pulls out and slowly pushes back in, and I try to follow his instructions but can't. I gag on his cock and cough as he pulls it free of my mouth and stares down at me.

"How often do you fail?"

"All the time," I murmur.

"Does it stop you from trying again?"

I press my lips together in a flat line before finally replying. "No."

"You gonna give up on this? You gonna quit?"

Let Mount win and prove I'm not capable of controlling his body like he controls mine? "No." I bite out the word.

"Good. Because you're almost there."

His hands cup my jaw again, and the softness and care with which he holds my face shocks me more than the fact that the goal I'm trying to accomplish is deep-throating him. But when it comes to Mount, proving a point is proving a point, regardless of the context.

As he presses forward with his dick again, I breathe through my nose and swallow, taking it all until my nose presses against the hard plane of his stomach.

His eyes light with triumph, but it's different from before. It takes me another stroke and swallow of his cock to realize it's not out of smug victory, but *pride*.

He continues to fuck my face, several strokes shallow and then one deep, each time alerting me with a subtle pressure from his hands as if preparing me for what's coming next.

When I went to my knees before him, something

I swore I wouldn't do, my sole intent was to steal his power. But something else is happening here, and I can't put a name to it.

"You're gonna swallow every drop, hellion."

I dare him with my eyes to try to hold out, but he doesn't seem fazed by it. Instead, he fucks my mouth faster and faster, not going deep, but keeping his strokes shallow to focus on the tip of his cock. His hands never leave my face, even when he throws back his head and bellows as he spills down my throat.

I keep my end of the bargain and swallow every bit of it as he releases his hold and grips the edge of his desk to stay upright.

In that moment, I realize the game Mount is playing with me is more dangerous than he knows, because I just gained the advantage.

I almost brought the most powerful and feared man in this city to his knees, and I can't wait to do it again.

THIRTEEN

Mount

MY CELL PHONE BUZZES AGAIN AND AGAIN, NO doubt the Mexicans I hung up on in favor of teaching Keira to suck my dick, and I can't even bring myself to care.

I don't remember the last time I came that hard—outside of the times I've spilled in Keira's tight pussy with no condom. I've never trusted a woman's word that she's on birth control, but for some reason, I trust hers.

It would take me one phone call to verify, but I don't even feel the need to do that. Maybe because in some fucked-up universe, if I were to accidentally get Keira pregnant, it would give me an undeniable hold over her for life.

I vowed from an early age that I'd never bring a kid into this hell of a world. The consequences would be unthinkable. It wouldn't just be a weakness—it would be the ultimate sin, by far worse than anything I've ever done before.

Besides, what the fuck do I know about how to raise a kid, or how to love anyone? My entire life has revolved around control or the lack of it, and all I know is how to hold tight to the power I've fought to gain over so many years. I know I should use condoms from now on, but the thought of separating my dick from her hot pussy with a layer of latex has me gritting my teeth.

I don't want anything between us.

I know I'm in deeper than I should be, but I can't make myself pull back. What's more, I don't want to pull back.

When Keira stands in front of me, her tits heaving against the bustier while she tries to catch a breath, I cup her cheek again.

"Not bad, for a beginner."

She lifts a shaking hand to her face and draws all but her middle finger back before pressing a kiss to the pad of it, flipping me off again.

What would it be like to have her as compliant after sex as she is during?

A pipe dream, no doubt.

I reach out to snatch her wrist and force her hand down between her legs. Without breaking her defiant green gaze, I drag her finger over the drenched seam of her pussy.

"You feel that? You're soaked for me. Deny it all you want, but we both know the truth." Using her finger, I tap her piercing lightly, knowing it will drag her closer to the edge the fastest. "You think it's your turn to come?"

"Yes! I did what you wanted." Her response carries an undeniable edge of need.

I use her finger to tease her entrance. "And you think that entitles you to an orgasm?"

Her nod is swift, and I continue to torture her with her own finger, her breathy moans making my dick hard again already.

Before she can come, I yank her hand away and catch her other wrist, pinning both behind her back as she struggles against my hold.

"No. You don't get to come. That's what you get for being late."

"It was five minutes!"

"Five minutes or five hours, you were still late."

"But—"

"Give me one more excuse, and the only butt we're going to be talking about is the one filled with a plug right now. Actually, I think you're almost ready. One more size to go, and we're going to see if I can finally fit my fat cock in your ass."

FOURTEEN

Keira

HOW CAN MY NIPPLES BE HARD, MY PUSSY BE WET, and my hand itch to grab the lamp on his desk to bludgeon him to death all at the same time?

This man drives me absolutely insane. If I don't get away from him right now, I'll do something unthinkable.

Like lay yourself out on his desk and beg him to fuck you in exchange for whatever he wants, as long as he lets you come? I shove down my inner voice as I tug my wrists from Mount's grip.

Surprisingly, he lets me go.

I edge away from the desk, trying to gauge his expression. He's impossible to read.

"I assume you'd like to go to work today?" he asks.

Work. How the hell did I forget about work?

"Yes. Of course. There's always more to do there."

"That I understand."

It's strange to think about, but maybe it's the one

thing we have in common—we both run our own business. Or in his case, an empire. But then again, that's my goal too, for Seven Sinners to dominate the world whiskey market. My dad's plans were never so grand, nor were his father's or grandfather's, but I think bigger. I see what we could be, if only I had the right connections and the cash. That's part of how Brett sucked me in so easily. He made me believe that he shared my vision. He painted the picture of the future I wanted so badly, and I fell for it and him.

Brett.

The thought of him makes bile rise in my throat as I remember the note on the first appointment reminder that popped up this morning. *Your prior appointment has been handled.*

I take a few more steps away from Mount before I voice the question I originally rushed to his door to have answered. "How did you— What did you—" I stumble over the words, unable to get them right. "What happened with Brett?"

Mount's unreadable expression shifts into that granite-like hardness I've come to know well. "You won't ever have to worry about him again."

"But what does that mean?"

My voice rises because this isn't something I can just let go. Last night, seeing the man I thought I'd laid to rest standing at my doorway was the ultimate shock. I've never before fainted in my life, but I hit the floor like a bag of grain.

When I came to, Brett stood over me, his weight shifting from foot to foot as he crossed and uncrossed his arms. The barrel of the gun in his hand constantly moved as he used the back of his hand to rub his nose, sniffling like he had a cold. I've never recognized the signs before, but after what Magnolia told me, I knew that he was on drugs. Cocaine, I assumed. I don't have the kind of experience to know if it was something else, and thank God for that.

His face, once so familiar, was thinner, his cheeks hollowed and the dark circles under his eyes so prominent, they looked like mine when I wake up without washing the eye makeup from my face after a night out.

It didn't take long for him to tell me exactly what he wanted. Money. And the penalty for not following through? Killing my entire family.

Did he scare the frigging hell out of me? Yes. Did it piss me off that people kept threatening people I love? Absolutely.

He laid out his plan and I promised to comply because, hell, I've already sold my body for them, what was giving up money I didn't even know I had? At this point, it seemed there was nothing I wouldn't sacrifice to save them, not that they'd ever know.

When Brett left, it was with a sickening laugh before he shut the door.

"Too bad you were so fucking awful at running a business. I would've stuck around longer if that place hadn't been going down the tubes. Then again, you were a terrible lay. Not sure I could've stomached sticking my dick in your frigid pussy again."

I wanted to scream. Rage. Tell him that the only reason I've done the most impulsive thing of my life—eloping with him—was because I thought he was the one to give me everything I ever wanted the night of the masquerade. But I didn't. He was already unstable, and I wasn't about to make it worse.

I just wanted him gone, and now I want to know if he's gone for good.

"Did you kill him?" I put the question to Mount point-blank.

He lowers himself back into his desk chair, laces his fingers together, and rests them on his desk. "Haven't you realized by now that I will never answer that question, no matter how many times you ask it or who it is you ask about?"

My spine stiffens at his non-answer, and I stalk across the room again until only his desk separates us. "Don't you think I deserve to know if I'm really a widow this time?"

He looks down at the desk, and I follow his every movement. His thumbs tap together three times before he raises his head and meets my gaze.

"I could take you before any judge or preacher in this city, and you'd be my wife in less than ten minutes."

I rock back on the skyscraper heels, my mind spinning at his answer, and sputter out a retort. "Because you probably have something on all of them, and they'd do whatever you say. Isn't that how life works for the infamous Lachlan Mount?"

He unlaces his fingers, presses both palms to the desk, and rises out of his chair just enough to bring us eye level. "You're exactly fucking right about that." His voice is deep and rough, as though daring me to challenge him again.

I open my mouth to snap something back, but he keeps speaking.

"Don't question me when I tell you that if I married you today, you'd be legally mine."

It's not the implication that he killed my husband or had him killed sometime between last night and this morning that sends me stumbling back a step. No, it's the very thought of Mount dragging me before a judge or priest to marry him that scares the living hell out of me.

I find my balance and my backbone, squaring my shoulders. "Good thing we both know that will never happen."

That familiar smug smile tugs at the edges of his mouth. "Never say never, Keira."

I tear my gaze away from his and spin around, needing to get out of the room as fast as humanly possible on these skyscraper heels. When I reach the doorway, he speaks again.

"Your clothes for work are in my closet. Keep the plug in for another hour, and don't stay at the distillery too late. I've got plans for you tonight."

FIFTEEN

Mount

KEIRA SLAMS THE OFFICE DOOR BEHIND HER, AND the grin I've been fighting spreads across my face. No closing the door with a quiet and meek click from my Irish hellion.

I reach for my cell phone and scroll through the messages I've missed and my secure emails, but I can't concentrate on a single fucking word. My gaze keeps dropping to the floor where she knelt before me, and then shifts to the surface of the desk I bent her across.

Keira's scent still hangs in the air, and my concentration is well and truly fucked. I shove out of my chair with a disgusted grunt before crossing the room to engage the lock on the door—which I still find laughable she tried to pick with a hairpin—before turning to the left to trigger the hidden exit.

As soon as I step into the interior hallway, the tension riding me lessens a few degrees. I force myself to head for my other office since my library is out of the question because of her.

I'm almost to the entrance when I spot J heading in the same direction.

"Is everything okay, boss? You haven't been answering your messages."

"What do you want?"

"There are some very angry Mexicans who demand you call them immediately. The situation from last night has turned into a mess."

I use my thumbprint to disengage the lock. When the interior door to my office slides open, we both step into the room. "I don't need to explain shit to them, and they don't get to make demands. This is my city."

J takes a seat across from the desk. "How long do you think you can keep them under your thumb? The cartels aren't going to let you maintain control forever."

"*Let me maintain control?* Is that what you think is going on here?"

"They're gaining even more power. No one else has kept them in line like you, but what if the balance shifts?"

I curl my hands into fists and plant them on my desk. "The balance isn't shifting. I keep them in line because no one else has the leverage on them that I do. The fact that they don't make a move without my say-so isn't a fucking accident. You know that."

J has been with my crew long enough to know more about the secrets I keep and the resulting blackmail than anyone, except possibly V.

"I'm just saying, we need to be smart. Maybe not pissing them off by hanging up on them after you killed a lieutenant might be a good plan next time."

"And you think kowtowing to them would do more to show that I don't give a flying fuck what power they think they have? This is *my city*. I make the rules."

J leans back in the chair. "Don't take this the wrong way, boss—"

"You know I kill most people who start a sentence like that."

"Yeah, well, I wouldn't be the loyal friend I am if I didn't tell you that you've been distracted lately."

The distraction being referred to is Keira, and it pisses me off that J dares to bring her up. "Tread lightly."

With both palms in the air, J attempts to placate me. "I'm not saying it's bad, I'm just saying . . . she's got a hold on you. I'm worried she's fucking with your head. The others, it was like they didn't exist once you moved on, but this one seems different. If I see it, who else sees it? You've stayed on top because people don't just fear and respect you, but because you've made sure you have no weakness to exploit."

I narrow my eyes on my second-in-command. "I still don't have a fucking weakness to exploit, and this subject is closed."

J nods, respect in the movement. "Yes, sir. When you have some free time, there are several decisions waiting for you to sign off on. Let me know when you want to go through them."

The implication that I'm not staying on top of my business because of Keira infuriates me. "Right now. Let's knock it all out. Neither of us is leaving this room

until every single outstanding item has been covered. You think I'm distracted? You're fucking wrong.
Nothing has changed."

Even as I say the words, I know I'm lying.

Everything has changed.

SIXTEEN

Keira

I STILL HAVE EXACTLY ONE OUTFIT FROM WHICH TO choose, but the only difference this time? It's in Mount's closet. I suppose I could attempt to turn one of his custom-tailored shirts into some kind of fashion statement, using a fancy tie for a belt.

The thought crosses my mind for all of two seconds before I take the black-and-white striped dress from the hanger and slip into it. Once again, it's designer, expensive as hell, and fits like a dream. Oh, and the accompanying lingerie actually includes a thong and a beautiful lace bra this time, so that's a plus.

When I open the door to Mount's suite, V is waiting outside. He silently delivers me to work—sans hood—and I keep the plug in for the prescribed hour before sneaking into my bathroom to remove it. Then I bury myself in work and deal with one thing after another until I can almost forget this morning.

Almost.

I'm a widow.

It shouldn't be a startling realization considering I've believed that for months, but knowing that it's only now true is a completely different situation.

I should feel sorrow, or *something*, for the fact that Mount "took care of" Brett sometime after he left last night and before I woke up this morning. But, truthfully, all I feel is relief.

How terrible of a person does that make me?

I can't even blame it on Mount's influence, because after my first encounter with him in this office, I remember thinking that if Brett were still alive, I'd kill him myself for putting me in this situation. And last night, when he was describing how he'd kill my family, I wanted to rip the gun from his hand and unload every bullet into his chest, except for maybe saving a single shot to put right between his eyes.

I brace my elbows on my desk and drop my head into the cradle of my hands.

Who am I?

I suck in a wild breath and lift my gaze to the ceiling. I don't recognize myself anymore. I'm sitting in my office, the one I've dreamed about having since I was a little girl, wearing clothes selected for me by a man who murdered my husband or had him murdered, and instead of going to the police to tell them what happened, I'm thinking about how badly I wanted him to fuck me on his desk this morning.

What is wrong with me?

It's a question I can't answer, so I go back to my pile of work, pretending I'm not being torn apart by a moral crisis I'm pretty sure is going to land me in hell because I can't drum up a single bit of remorse.

I lose track of time, probably because my last conference call drones on for an hour longer than necessary as I negotiate the preliminaries of a supply contract before turning over the details to the lawyers to draft.

"So, we'll see you in Dublin in a couple days to celebrate the deal in person at GWSC?" Roy asks. He's a premium organic-grain supplier I need as a backup to my primary so I'm not sole-sourced.

GWSC is the Global Whiskey and Spirits Conference, an event I've wanted to attend since my dad went with my grandfather when I was twenty. After that, Dad said it was an expense the company couldn't justify, and since I've taken the helm, that's continued to be the case.

"I was hoping to get a ticket last minute, but the event I've got coming up is going to change those plans." My answer is complete bullshit. I haven't even attempted to register because it would be the height of irresponsibility to jaunt off to my dream conference when I can't make payroll. At least, I couldn't before Mount intervened.

Regardless, I'm not about to admit that Seven Sinners is having money issues to a potential supplier.

"That's disappointing. They've got some heavy hitters coming in. We're really excited to attend because we've doubled our grain output this year and have a lot of interest on the supply side."

I read between the lines of his comment. "I hope

that's not your way of telling me you're going to play hardball on these negotiations, Roy. You know we made a deal." I say it with a smile in my voice but grip the pen in my hand, using it to make a stabbing motion toward the doodle-edged notepad on my desk.

Roy guffaws. "Of course not. You know me. Man of my word."

"Good to know that there are still men like you who have unquestionable credibility. That's such a rare commodity these days. Hopefully, I'll see you at GWSC next year."

We hang up, promising to get the lawyers going on the drafting of the contract, and I look at the doodles on my notepad around the contract terms.

I'm getting a good deal, as long as his lawyers don't screw it all up when they draft it. I swear they love to make simple things complicated.

My mind rewinds the last few minutes of our conversation about GWSC, and I let myself dream for a minute. I pull up the registration website on my computer and read over the details.

If I could go, I would have a shot at some of the best networking of my life. It could be the difference between Seven Sinners thriving like I want, or continuing to eke out an existence. My father would say I'm an idiot for even considering it, but he came from a different generation. Work hard. Play hard. Move on.

I don't want to continue the family tradition that way. I want to build a whiskey empire.

God, listen to me. I sound like Mount.

I shove away from my desk and stand, my

shoulders, neck, and back protesting how long I've been sitting, and my stomach growls.

Good thing I own a restaurant. I step out of my office to find Temperance striding down the hall in my direction.

"Oh, good. I thought you forgot."

My mind races to figure out what she could possibly be talking about. "Forgot what?"

"Shit, you did forget. That's okay. It's fine. You're not late. I was coming to get you so you wouldn't be." She leads me in the direction of the elevator, and I still don't have a single clue what she's talking about.

"What am I missing?"

The elevator door opens and we step inside. Temperance hits the button for the top floor. "Your meeting with the head of the tourism board."

"Oh crap!" She's right. I completely forgot.

"This is kind of a big deal, Keira. I was hoping you'd be excited instead of writing it off completely."

I open my mouth to tell her that my life has been a little chaotic ever since Lachlan Mount decided I was sufficient payment for a debt. And then there's the whole *he killed my husband* thing that I'm apparently not upset about, which also threw me off my game. I snap my teeth together with a clack, because there's no way in hell I can tell her any of this.

I can't tell anyone, except maybe Magnolia. She lives in the world I'm partially inhabiting, and would understand more than anyone else.

"I'm not writing it off. Truly. It's just been a crazy few days."

"It's okay. You'll be fine. It totally falls in line with the thing I've been telling you we should do," she says.

"What thing?" I ask, acknowledging to myself that I'm basically a shitty CEO today, but I'm giving myself a pass.

"The tours and the gift shop. We need to bring more people through. Get them personally invested in Seven Sinners. If they see how we make it, meet the people who are responsible for bringing the world's best whiskey to life, and then taste it right afterward, they're a hell of a lot more likely to become customers for life. It'll be the experience they never forget. The one they post about on social media with awesome hashtags. We need this, Keira."

She hands me a printed sheet of paper, and I stare down at the bullet points.

"Oh. That thing."

I inhale through my nose and exhale slowly, because I know there's merit to what she's saying. She's absolutely, one hundred percent right. But my dad went ballistic after he found out I started a construction project to create the restaurant as soon as he signed the company over to me. If I start bringing tour groups through the facility and showing them exactly how we make our whiskey, he'll lose his goddamned mind and be out of retirement so fast, my head will spin.

Our process isn't crazy unusual, because all whiskey is made in a somewhat similar process, but we have several special steps that are proprietary. Bringing tours through would put the secrecy surrounding them in jeopardy.

"You know I'm right," Temperance says as the elevator door opens on the restaurant level, and holds the button to keep it open as I step out.

"I know. But my dad—"

"Your dad isn't in charge anymore. How many times do you say that to people on a weekly basis?" My silence is all the answer she needs to continue. "You took on a massive construction project without his approval because you believed in it. This isn't even that big of a deal."

"But our intellectual property—"

"Will be safe. We can structure the tour in a way that everything works."

"What about liability? The lawyers would lose their shit."

Temperance rolls her eyes. "Stop giving me excuses. Go wine and dine the head of the tourism board, and tell him all the reasons this upcoming addition to the Seven Sinners distillery is going to be one of New Orleans' newest and most memorable attractions."

"And I thought I was the CEO here." I shoot back the reply with a grin as she releases the elevator button and the doors slide to close.

"Oh, and just because I know you forgot, the new president of the board's name is Jeff Doon. He said you two know each other?" Her voice goes quiet as she disappears from sight.

She also misses my mouth dropping open.

Jeff Doon was my high school boyfriend. The boy I lost my virginity to down by the levee after senior prom. The experience was the world's biggest cliché, and just as underwhelming as one would expect.

I haven't seen him in years, but he sent a card and flowers to the memorial service for Brett, telling me he was around if I ever needed anything.

I'm two steps into the restaurant when I catch sight of him. He sees me at the exact same moment, practically bouncing off the seat of the booth to stand with his arms outstretched.

Oh, sweet Jesus.

I don't even want to think about what Mount's going to do when he finds out.

I'm going to have to lie. There's no other option. Or Jeff might be "taken care of" by tomorrow too.

SEVENTEEN

Mount

Mount: Where the hell are you?
    V: Still waiting on the package.
    Mount: Where the hell is she?
    V: Inside.

I pull up the app on my phone to double-check the location of the tracker built into Keira's necklace, which surprisingly, she hasn't tried to remove with bolt cutters yet. Maybe she realized its utility when we were able to find her in her apartment.

Or maybe the idea of bolt cutters hasn't crossed her mind yet. That's probably the more likely answer.

The beacon shows she's still in the building, but not in her basement office. I manipulate the app to give me a better view of the building. Technology is a magical thing, because now I know she's in the restaurant.

I glance at the time. It's almost seven thirty.

Snatching my second cell off the desk, the one I use

to communicate with Keira and no one else, I shoot her a text.

> MOUNT: *You need to be on your way out the door in two minutes or V will be in to collect you.*

I wait to see some indication that she's read the text, but there's nothing.

Fuck two minutes. I don't wait for anyone, and Keira should have been home hours ago, as far as I'm concerned.

Switching phones again, I give new orders to V.

> MOUNT: *Go up to the restaurant. Find out what's keeping her and escort her down. I'm done waiting.*
> V: *Will do, boss.*
> MOUNT: *Let me know when you have her secured and are on your way back.*

After my conversation with J, and the suggestion that Keira has become a weakness that others will surely notice, I'm even more on guard. The car that V drives her to and from work in every day has bullet-resistant glass and is armor plated. It's heavy as fuck, which is why I never drive it. I value speed, power, and aesthetics, and have an extensive collection of both supercars and American muscle. I don't discriminate; I just collect them all.

Someone would have to have a death wish to try to take me out. I know the cartel is unhappy, but I also have information that would destroy them from the inside out, leaving them struggling to pull themselves together as an organization for years. I'm not stupid. I don't make a move without considering all the consequences.

Or, at least, I never did until *her*.

J was right about one thing. Keira is different. She fights me at every turn. Her submission is never certain, but when it's given, it's that much sweeter. Her body burns as hot as the fire in her eyes, and it's that inferno I'm addicted to.

Fuck.

J's right. I need to get my shit together and figure out how to compartmentalize like I always have. Keira's presence can take over my personal life, but my business requires my full concentration.

I need to do a full security sweep and make sure that no one has taken advantage of my momentary distractedness. Everyone in my organization needs their files updated to ensure they haven't developed any weaknesses that would allow someone to turn them against me. And it needs to happen now.

I shoot a text to J with the order, and get a quick response.

J: Good thinking, boss. Who do you want to use?

We have two investigators who would rather fall on their sword than miss a single piece of information. Their loyalty has been proven like everyone else's, one more recently than the other. The third investigator who missed Brett Hyde's former marriage certificate has been forcibly retired.

> MOUNT: *Use them both. Independently. I don't want them to know they're both on the job. Send every updated file to me. I'm reviewing them personally.*
> J: *Yes, sir. I'll get it going.*

As soon as I've turned away from my desk, my phone buzzes again with a text, and it's not the phone I used to send a message to Keira.

> V: *She's meeting with some guy. You want me to get her or wait?*

The fuck?

I hit the button on my desk to bring my monitors out of their hidden compartments and pull up the camera feeds of Seven Sinners restaurant.

I zoom in on the booth where I see Keira's fiery red hair and the man seated on the opposite side. He's reaching across the table, like he wants to grab her hands, but she pulls hers back and tucks them in her lap.

I respond to V.

> MOUNT: *Who the fuck is this guy?*
> V: *Don't know.*

And I know V sure as hell won't ask anyone because

he hasn't spoken in over a decade.

I grab a screenshot of the guy's face and shoot it to J.

> MOUNT: *I need a name and background on him. Now.*
> J: *On it, boss.*

My second-in-command's computer skills are off the charts. After what I paid for an MIT education, they should be.

It takes less than three minutes before I get a response.

> J: *Check your email.*

I pull up the secured app, and each word I read pisses me off even more.

My phone vibrates with a new text.

> V: *You want me to get her?*
> MOUNT: *No. I'll handle this myself.*

EIGHTEEN

Keira

'VE BEEN TRYING TO WRAP THIS DINNER UP AS FAST as humanly possible, but I feel with each second that passes, there's another strike against me. Or worse, against Jeff.

Scar has to be waiting outside. I wasn't supposed to work late.

Mount will know.

I'm not naive enough to think that there's any way in hell he won't have Jeff's name, address, Social Security number, and complete bio by the time Scar delivers me back to my cage.

Mount will probably even know what brand condom Jeff used when he screwed me—terribly, I might add—in the back of his dad's Caddy when I was seventeen.

"I'll take another look at the presentation your assistant sent in advance, and will wait for you to let us know when you're ready to rock. I think this could be really great, Keira. We could use another attraction off Bourbon Street for people who don't just want to party. This would be educational, and they can taste some fantastic hometown whiskey."

He raises his glass to mine, and I force the smile to stay on my face as I clink my glass with his, sending up a prayer for his safety as I down the contents.

"I hate to end this dinner, and the great conversation, but I have another appointment I have to get to. Thank you so much, Jeff. Temperance will be in touch as soon as we have the details sorted out for you."

I stand up, smoothing my skirt, and Jeff rises from his side of the booth and steps forward to wrap me in a hug.

"It's good to see you again, Keira. It's been too long. I hope next time we can do a little more catching up instead of just talking business."

I nod because that's the only response I can give, hoping I'm not signing his death warrant. "We'll definitely be in touch. You should stay and have another drink. On me."

"Maybe you could reschedule your next appointment and join me?"

"Unfortunately, I can't."

The wattage of Jeff's smile dims a few degrees, but I keep mine firmly in place as I give him a final nod. I turn and cross the restaurant floor, blindly smiling at other patrons, but don't stop to speak to anyone before I hit the elevator.

It seems to take forever to descend to the basement level, and my foot taps impatiently in the slightly less provocative shoes Mount left in the closet for me today.

When the doors finally slide open, I rush down the hall and shove open my office door, mumbling to myself. "I just need to get my purse, get to Mount, and explain—"

"Explain what, exactly?"

The familiar deep voice comes out of the darkness. My heart hammers in my chest, and I slam my hand over it.

"Jesus Christ, you scared the hell out of me."

"I should. Because you have thirty seconds to explain why you're having dinner with your high-school fuck buddy instead of returning early like I ordered."

"It wasn't like that—"

Mount flips on the desk lamp, reminding me of the first time I saw him sitting in my chair. Then, terror like I'd never experienced raced in my veins. Tonight, I definitely feel fear, but not for myself. For someone else.

"Get over here."

As I cross the cracked floor, each click of my heels seems to echo in the otherwise silent room. "He's not—"

"I changed my mind. I don't want a fucking explanation. I want your ass in front of me right now." The chair scrapes against the concrete as Mount shoves away from the desk and stands.

I clamp my lips shut, not wanting to piss him off, but also not willing to let Jeff suffer consequences he had no clue existed. My feet move at Mount's command as I explain anyway.

"It was business. He's innocent, I swear to God.

Leave him alone."

I don't realize I'm within arm's reach until Mount wraps a hand around my wrist, pulling me against his chest.

"Innocent? Do you really think his thoughts were virtuous when he looked at you? Not fucking likely."

"It was business," I say again. "Please don't hurt him. He did nothing to deserve it."

Mount reaches up and grips my chin. He stares into my eyes as though he's peering into my mind to find the real truth.

"I swear to you, I'm telling the truth."

He searches my face, and he must find something that appeases him because he releases his hold on me. "I believe you."

His words send shock waves rolling through me. "You do?"

"You're a shitty liar at best. And I saw the footage. He might want to fuck you, but he wasn't threatening you. He's safe."

I breathe a sigh of relief. "Thank—"

Before I can get the word *you* out, Mount spins me around and grips the back of my neck to press me forward until my breasts touch my desk.

"But that doesn't mean I don't feel like reminding you that I'm the only man who touches you." He leans down, his words a rumble against my ear. "You. Are. Mine."

I release another harsh breath, but it doesn't have anything to do with fear. In fact, I should be ashamed at how fast my body switches gears. At my very core—my deepest, darkest secret depths—this is what I've always wanted. *Always*. A man who wants me with this intense ferocity and makes damn sure I know that I belong to him and only him.

But why does it have to be this man?

It's a question I have no answer to, yet I can't help but mouth off to him anyway. Mount expects nothing less from me. And for some reason, my rebellion always makes things hotter.

"You don't own me."

Mount yanks the hem of my dress up and tugs my thong down. "That's where you're fucking wrong."

His palm slaps my right cheek, the smack just hard enough to sting but not enough to cause true pain. Instead, a bloom of heat follows, and my inner muscles clench at the sensation I've come to crave. Mount delivers smack after smack before stopping to massage my ass and the decadent burn he caused.

I try to stifle the moan, but it escapes against my will. His hand slides between my legs, and he growls at the wetness he finds.

"You can deny it all you want, but we both know you love this. Unlike your smart little mouth, your body always tells the truth."

I can't say anything because he's right. I do love it. When he releases his hold on me for a moment, I lift up, but he quickly grips my shoulder.

"I didn't say you could move. We aren't even close to done here."

Shivers ripple across my skin, and my nipples pebble in my bra as he pushes me back down. This is the hold of the man from that night at the masquerade. The one who took me up against a wall, never letting me turn around. The man who gave me everything I needed, and because of that night, I thought I eloped with him.

Now I know I was wrong. I was wrong about everything . . . except this.

This is what I want. What I need.

The hiss of Mount's zipper breaks the silence between the hammering beats of my heart, making me anticipate his touch. He pushes a thick finger inside me, circling my piercing until I'm writhing on my desk. Then he pulls it away to rim my asshole.

"Where's the plug?"

"I took it out like you said."

"Where is it?"

I lick my lips, debating how I'm going to answer the question. While I'm contemplating, he squeezes a still-burning cheek of my ass.

"In the bottom left drawer with the lube. I cleaned it before I wrapped it up and hid it."

"Good girl. Because now you're going to find out what it's like to be fucked with both your holes filled."

Another rush of moisture floods my center. Another secret dirty fantasy of mine.

He releases his hold and opens the desk drawer I just described. A few seconds later, lube coats my asshole, and he slides the plug inside as he teases my pussy. It takes every ounce of self-control I have not to writhe on the desk and beg.

Mount grips my hair and turns my face to the side

to study me. He shakes his head, his gaze black and his smile arrogant. "You were fucking made for me."

With that shocking declaration, he fits his cock against my entrance and pushes the head inside.

"Oh my God." My voice comes out a harsh whisper at the intense fullness, but Mount's groan covers my words as he pushes inside another inch.

"My cock barely fits in your tight cunt with that plug. Jesus fucking Christ."

I'm losing my mind, pleasure overtaking any rational thought as Mount fills me slowly and proceeds to fuck me thoroughly, bent over my desk, until I'm a mess of pleas and moans.

My orgasm rips through me moments before he comes, and then the only sound in my office is the mingled sound of our labored breathing.

NINETEEN

Keira

EXPECTED TO ENJOY THE AFTERGLOW FROM ONE OF the most powerful orgasms of my life for longer than two minutes, but no, that's not how things worked out. Instead, I fume the entire way back to Mount's compound.

After the crazy, intense encounter in my office, he walked me out to the car and shut me in the backseat without another word of explanation beyond *Plans changed. I have business.*

Plans changed because he already fucked me and now he doesn't need me again tonight? I want to beat against something, but the back of Scar's seat isn't going to satisfy me.

"I wish you would freaking talk, because maybe you could help me understand how his head works. If he thinks tossing me in the back of the car is somehow a good move, he's beyond wrong."

I hate how my voice shakes, and tell myself it's

anger and not the threat of tears.

How can I want him so badly? How can I possibly think he's the one who can give me everything I've ever needed physically? Well, he's missing an important freaking piece of the puzzle, because he doesn't know how to give a damn about anyone emotionally.

When Scar delivers me to Mount's suite, I storm inside, heading for the bathroom, ready to wash off the scent that I can't get out of my head. A noise from the closet catches my attention, and I spin around with a screech.

"Who the hell are you?" I demand.

A gray-haired older man with a matching moustache and wearing a pinstripe suit stands in the closet holding the handle of what appears to be a clothes steamer. "Oh, so sorry. I was informed you'd be away for the evening, and I had time to situate things."

That's when I realize what else has changed in the closet. Instead of being full of Mount's suits and shirts, evenly spaced across all the bars, it's been reorganized. A third of the closet now contains women's clothes. Dresses, skirts, blouses, slacks, and more.

My shock must be evident on my face because the older man hangs the steamer handle on the machine, leaving a gorgeous black dress partially wrinkled.

"I'm G, Mr. Mount's tailor. And I suppose if we were in England, maybe something of a valet. I attend to his wardrobe, and now yours."

I blink a few times, staring at the gorgeous clothes hanging in Mount's closet. The man, G, continues speaking, even though I don't respond.

"I apologize if I frightened you. That was not my intent. I'll just get out of the way and be off for the evening."

He packs up the equipment with efficiency, like he's done it dozens of times, and heads toward where I stand in the doorway. Somehow, I have a feeling he doesn't normally use the regular entrance, but instead some secret one I still don't know about.

I haven't found words to respond to him yet, but I back away so he can pass. Instead of striding out, he pauses in the doorway of the closet.

"Miss, are you okay?"

I nod, but his look of concern stays in place. I can tell he wants to ask again, but he picks up the machine and exits the room. I don't move until I hear the outer door close.

Once I'm sure he's gone, I walk into the closet, reach out a hand, and run it along the edges of all the sumptuous fabrics. They're all beautiful, but that means nothing.

Up until this moment, I've gotten one outfit at a time. *One day at a time.* Everything about that equated to a temporary situation. This full wardrobe doesn't say *temporary.* It says something completely different.

My entire body shakes as I slide down the edge of the center island in the closet until my butt hits the carpeted floor. I wrap my arms around my knees, trying to stop the trembling, but it's impossible.

All the emotions of tonight rush over me in a tsunami that I'm not prepared to handle.

What is happening to my life?

This arrangement is supposed to end, and things are supposed to go back to how they were before I knew Mount existed. In the beginning, when I demanded an end date, he wouldn't give me one.

I bite my lip as tears burn behind my eyes.

What if he never lets me go?

I swipe at my lids as I comprehend what that would mean.

A complete loss of my independence.

Never again being able to be honest with my family.

The death of all my dreams.

How long until I lose the very essence of what makes me *me*?

I thought I could handle him, thought I was strong enough to keep it all together. But I've never been more wrong in my life, and it's going to cost me everything.

I drop my forehead to my knees and let the tears stream down. If I were a decent human being, tonight I'd be mourning the actual death of my husband.

Instead, I'm mourning the loss of my own life.

TWENTY

Mount

WHEN I TELL KEIRA MY PLANS FOR THE EVENING have changed because I have business to attend to and send her home with V, I'm only partially lying.

Confusion lines her features, but it doesn't matter. I have to get away from her. J's words still echo through my head, and I know that what happened tonight shifted things even further in the opposite direction from where they should be going.

Compartmentalization? Fuck, I'll be lucky if I can ever look at *any* desk without getting an instant hard-on from picturing Keira bent over it.

Despite the lie I told her, too much truth was spoken in her office tonight. She loves what I give her and is on the verge of admitting it, even though she doesn't have to. I see it in her every reaction. Her body responds to me like nothing I've ever seen. She was made for me—I knew it the night of the masquerade. That's why I had to have her again, only to be denied for too long.

Work. That's what I need.

Even though the casino isn't nearly as busy as it will be later tonight, I walk the floor, stopping to watch dealers flip cards across the green felt of table after table, and observe the spinning roulette wheel as the ball clatters across the black, red, and green numbers. At the craps table, a call girl blows on the dice for a player before he throws them, and groans when he loses everything.

I shake a few people's hands and watch their mouths moving, but don't hear their words. I'm too distracted. The lights and sounds of the casino used to fascinate me, but they're not enough to keep my mind off her.

In less than ten minutes, I could be in my bedroom, preferably with Keira pinned beneath me, her red hair spread across my pillow again. Except this time, her green eyes would be snapping at me in rebellion until I buried myself inside her. Then they'd go soft, wanting, needing, *begging* for what only I can give her.

As my dick jerks at the vision, I shove the thought away. *Because that's not what I'm going to do.* I'm getting out of here.

I duck into the security control room, remind them to keep an eye on a few specific guests, and leave through a sliding panel in the wall.

I take the long way around, headed for a garage on the north side of my complex. Tonight, I need a drive to clear my head, and nothing does a better job of that than my Chevelle.

As I navigate the maze of secret hallways to get there, I spot a familiar figure heading toward his own rooms.

"G?"

The old man's head comes up and he pauses. "Sir? Do you require my services?"

"No. How did it go tonight?"

"I was able to finish steaming almost everything, but Ms. Kilgore returned sooner than anticipated, so I still have to finish the job. It'll be done tomorrow, however." He pauses before adding, "She seemed quite shocked when she saw the closet. Even more than shocked. Upset, really."

G is one of the very few people I trust, so I ask, "How upset?"

"Very. It seems like a warning might have been in order."

Most women, at least in my experience, would be thrilled to receive an expensive designer wardrobe like I had G put together for Keira. It shouldn't surprise me at all that her response would be the exact opposite.

"I'll deal with her."

G nods again and his lips press together, disappearing beneath his gray mustache.

"What? I can tell you want to say something else."

He takes his time, as though considering his words carefully. "She seems different from the others, sir. All of this seems different."

It's almost an exact recitation of what J said earlier.

I open my mouth to tell G that she's not different,

it's just the circumstances. The debt. That's the only reason I'm doing this. But he's one of the few people who can tell when I'm lying. So instead, I go with the truth.

"She is. All of it is. And I don't know what the fuck I'm doing."

I don't admit weakness. I always exude absolute control. You don't retain power like I have without it. But G is different. His loyalty is unquestioned.

"Then might I share a suggestion, sir?"

"Go ahead."

"She seems like the type of woman that needs to be handled with more care."

"I haven't hurt her." My tone takes on a sharp edge.

G shakes his head. "No, no, I would never imply that. What I mean is . . . you know she's different. That means you have to treat her differently."

I jam my hands into my hair. "I am. That's the whole fucking problem."

"Respectfully, sir, you're missing my point."

"Then just say it, old man. Lay it out, because it's obvious I'm not picking up on the subtleties here."

"Have you ever had to woo a woman?"

I look at him like he's just asked me for a dime bag. "Woo?"

"Yes. Entice. Seduce, but not sexually—emotionally. Court her. Show her that she *is* different by giving her something she needs or wants."

I mull over his words as he continues to speak.

"If you think about it, coming from the outside into your world would be a very difficult transition, especially under these circumstances. The position you hold is not one that many can, and it carries great responsibilities and risk. Maybe you should show her that there are also advantages to your position. Persuade her that making this transition is not without reward."

I know what G is saying. At least, I think I do.

I've stripped all of Keira's control away, and she's fought me at every turn. Her fire is what drew me to her, but if I keep pushing, there's a chance I could snuff it out. And that's not what I want at all.

What the fuck do I want? G won't be able to answer that question, so there's no use making him stand here waiting in the hallway.

"Thank you. I appreciate your candor."

"Of course, sir. I am always at your service," G says, and continues down the hall.

His words have me thinking as much as J's did earlier, but their advice pushes me in opposite directions.

I head toward my garage, more intent than ever on getting the hell out of here so I can try to sort my head out somewhere that doesn't remind me of Keira Kilgore.

TWENTY-ONE

Mount

THE GROWL OF THE CHEVELLE'S ENGINE IS EXACTLY what I needed, but instead of driving around aimlessly, it takes me somewhere I haven't been in a while, and that's something I need to rectify. The majority of my life is lived in the shadows. People whisper my name, as if afraid saying it out loud will bring me to their doorstep. Sometimes, it does.

But luckily for me, there are a few places that border the shadows where I can go without being bothered and still make the connections necessary to continue to expand my empire. The Jackson Club is one of those places.

It's rumored it was started by Andrew Jackson himself in the early 1800s, but I couldn't care less about the club's history or pedigree. All I care about is that the membership is exclusive, and there's a known rule that it's neutral territory. A hitman could see his target in the club, and if he made a move, the penalty would be death. Every member has the right to enforce that rule. It's the only way to maintain order in the club and allow some of the most powerful men in the world to feel at ease behind its hallowed doors.

I've heard the waiting list to be granted entrance is years long, but a few things get you to the top in a hurry—like a shitload of money, a blueblood pedigree, or some kind of celebrity status. Luckily for me, I own this town. They would never deny me entrance. In addition, the current manager is an acquaintance. Quade Buck keeps this club running efficiently, and no matter how many times I've tried to lure him away to run my casino, he turns me down. I can't blame him. I wouldn't want to work for me either. One major fuckup can easily cost someone their life.

Quade greets me from behind the bar as soon as I enter the dark-paneled room. The club is updated annually, and our dues reflect it. It's a masculine refuge from the outside world. Heavy wooden furniture dominates, and a tinge of cigar smoke not captured by the air-filtration system hangs in the air. Although I see plenty of familiar faces as I scan the large room, I choose to head in Quade's direction behind the bar first. A drink is definitely in order.

"When are you going to quit pulling shifts behind this bar? If you worked at my place, you wouldn't have to serve another drink as long as you live."

Quade's gruff laugh is the same response I get every time. "I don't mind slinging drinks. I'm not too proud to work. Besides, this way I get to keep my finger on the pulse of the club and what's happening with everyone in it. You drinking tonight?"

"Absolutely."

When Quade turns to grab what he knows is my preferred brand of Scotch, a bottle on the shelf catches my eye. *Seven Sinners whiskey.*

Fuck, she even followed me here.

Quade follows my gaze in the mirror toward it, missing nothing. "You changing it up tonight?" He shifts his hand to wrap around the neck of the Seven Sinners bottle, his eyebrows raised in question.

It's on the tip of my tongue to say that I've already had the best Seven Sinners has to offer tonight, but I bite it back. "No. I want exactly what I always have."

Quade eyes me with interest as he grabs the Scotch and pours three fingers, neat. When he slides it across the bar, he leans against the thick, aged wood. "What brings you in? It's been a few months since you've been around."

"Been wrapped up with a few issues."

He pushes off the bar and crosses his arms. "Issues? Thought men at your level didn't have those."

A huff that's half laugh, half grunt escapes my lips. "Wouldn't that be nice. I've got them handled. No other option."

"Scorched earth, right? That's what you're known for."

"Doesn't work all the time."

Quade tosses the towel in the sink and watches me for a few moments before speaking again. "Word around the club is that V has been spending a lot of time driving back and forth between your compound

149

and a certain distillery in town." He nods to the bottle of Seven Sinners whiskey on the shelf, as though his statement needs clarification.

J's warning was right. People are noticing and talking, and that's not good.

"Who the fuck cares where he's driving?"

Quade crosses his arms again. "Plenty of people, apparently. It's not like you're known for putting your mark on a local."

"What are they saying?" I need to know, because maybe scorched earth will become necessary to shut down any gossip.

"Everything from blackmail and extortion to kidnapping and indentured servitude." He eyes me carefully. "When it comes to you, I don't have a hard time believing any of it."

Relief surges through me because my obsession hasn't become part of the conversation.

When I don't reply, he asks, "You gonna tell me what's really going on, Mount?"

I lift the glass of Scotch to my lips and take a sip. Immediately, I wish I'd picked the whiskey.

What the hell is she doing to me?

"Does it matter?"

He shrugs. "Call it curiosity. No one could believe when Brett Hyde conned his way into that family. There's been more than one guy in the club who definitely wasn't sad to see her come back on the market."

I bite back the urge to tell him she's not on the fucking market, and won't be anytime soon. Before I have to come up with some suitable reply, a broad-shouldered man takes a stool one down from mine.

"I've been waiting for you to come out of your compound so I could talk you into selling me a piece of property you own in the Quarter. I don't do all that secret handshake and password bullshit it takes to track you down, but waiting isn't my forte either."

I turn to see Lucas Titan push his empty glass toward Quade.

"I'll take another, Buck." Turning back to me, Titan says, "So, what do you say? You willing to entertain offers?"

I don't have a damn clue what piece of property he's talking about, but it doesn't really matter. "Pretty sure you know I rarely sell anything I acquire."

"I get the *what's mine, I keep* mentality, but this is for my wife, so I'll make it worth your while."

"Which property?"

Titan accepts the refilled glass from Quade and takes a sip. "Don't worry, it's not part of your block. It's a couple streets over."

"What the hell does your wife want it for?" It's not vitally important to know, but in my position, more information is always better than less.

Quade disappears to the other end of the bar before Titan answers.

"She doesn't know she wants it yet. But she will. Her store's kicking ass. She's going to need to expand, and when she realizes she needs the space, I want it already lined up. It'll make for a hell of a surprise gift, but I know she'd never ask for it."

Titan's wife sounds a lot like one particular woman

I know. I dig through my memory to dredge up what I remember hearing about them when they hooked up.

"This is the wife you surprised with a wedding so she had no choice but to marry you on the spot?" I ask. The story made the rounds for months after it happened, since Titan might be the only man in this town with remotely close to as much money as me.

He takes another sip, but the grin on his face is clear. He answers when he finishes. "I did what I had to do to lock that woman down. She's stubborn as hell, and I've got no regrets."

"Clearly, it worked." I nod at his wedding ring. "Doesn't sound like a half-bad plan."

Titan eyes me with new interest. "Thinking about trying it yourself?"

"She'd just as soon murder me in my sleep at this point."

"Lachlan Mount with woman problems." Titan leans back on his stool, looking arrogant as hell. "Never thought I'd see the day."

"Fuck off."

Instead of dropping the subject, he laughs. "Let me give you a piece of unsolicited advice. Check your ego at the door. It isn't going to help you win this battle."

"You're right, definitely unsolicited."

I take another sip and make a snap decision. *Fuck it.* It's not like he's gonna talk. He's got something to lose if he pisses me off.

"Say I was having problems, and I check my ego. Then what?"

Titan gives me a nonchalant shrug. "Figure out

what she wants and then give it to her."

"Like it's that fucking easy," I reply with a harsh laugh.

"It is if you listen. She's gonna tell you. Maybe not outright, but you didn't get to where you are without being able to read between the lines."

I consider what he says. It sounds too simple.

Listen. Figure out what she wants. Give it to her.

Nothing with Keira could be that easy. Or could it? What the hell does she want most?

My inner voice wastes no time shooting back answers that piss me off. *Her freedom. Not to be tied to you by that debt.* Well, that's too fucking bad, because I'm not willing to give her either of those, so it has to be something else.

"So, you gonna sell me that building or what?"

By the time I leave the club, I've reached a deal with Titan to sell him the building, and my brain is already working out the answer to the million-dollar question.

How do I figure out what else Keira wants?

No matter what it is, I can get it for her. She's never seen the advantages of what my boundless resources bring to the table.

It's time to change that.

TWENTY-TWO

Keira

WHEN I WAKE UP THE NEXT MORNING, I GIVE myself the pep talk to end all pep talks. *I will not let him control me. He thinks he owns me, but he never will.* It gets repetitive enough to turn into a mantra.

The pillow beside mine has an impression indicating someone slept there last night, but I don't remember. If Mount did sleep here, he definitely didn't bother to wake me. Probably a good thing, because I had nail scissors on my nightstand that I might have used to stab him if he tried to touch me.

I come to a complete halt in the bathroom when the thought crosses my mind, and I stare in the mirror at myself.

I look the same, but *damn*, do I sound like a bloodthirsty crazy woman now or what? That definitely has to be Mount's influence, because I'm pretty sure I've never had a thought like that before. Maybe.

There was that time Jury sabotaged my date with the captain of the football team when I was in tenth grade, and instead of ending up at a party with him, his car died on the side of the road and we had to get help from a neighbor. I didn't know Jury had put sugar in his gas tank until the next day when I was complaining that he'd probably never take me out again because I was bad luck for his beloved Mustang.

When Jury met my gaze in the mirror and told me point-blank what she'd done, I grabbed the sharpest thing I could find, the pointy end of my makeup brush, and jabbed it in her direction.

"Why would you do that to me?"

"Because he told all his friends he was going to get you hammered and nail you. Then the next weekend, he was going after Imogen, and then me next month. He called it 'the Kilgore hat trick,' which apparently has become a challenge for a football player to pull off. But that shit ain't happening on my watch."

So, basically, only Mount and Jury make me stabby. And sometimes Imogen when she acts holier-than-thou. Thoughts of my sisters buoy my spirits, but also make me disheartened that we haven't stayed close as adults.

With that depressing thought, I take an age in the shower before venturing into the closet that almost broke me last night. I refuse to say it did break me, because that would be giving Mount too much power. I take my time choosing what to wear, and don the clothing like a suit of armor.

When I finish and step into the bedroom, I find

155

Mount leaning against the doorway to his office, which is usually locked. He's perfectly put together in a dark gray three-piece suit that makes his eyes look lighter than they normally do. He's also holding a black box.

Those damn black boxes.

"If that's another butt plug, I can tell you whose ass it's *not* going up this morning."

The edges of his mouth twitch but he doesn't smile . . . except with his eyes.

That's new. So is the humor in them as opposed to foreboding darkness.

"Don't tempt me to get the other box," he says. "Because I wasn't joking when I said there's one more."

Okay, so it's not a sex toy.

"What is it?"

He holds it out. "A gift."

"I don't need anything else added to my debt, thank you very much." I stand straight, sounding like a stuck-up bitch, but I can't help it. It's my only defense against him.

The humor fades from his eyes, but he doesn't start ordering me around immediately like I expected.

"It's not. Hence the word *gift.*" He walks toward me, shoves the box into my hands, and walks through the bedroom and out the door before I can respond.

I stare at the box like it contains all the mysteries of the universe, because honestly, that's about as good a guess as I have right now.

Carefully, I lift the lid and look inside.

It's a contract. Between an entity I don't recognize and Seven Sinners for the purchase of six thousand cases a year of our most expensive whiskeys.

What the hell?

Six thousand cases? I quickly do the math in my head. That would give me enough breathing room for a couple of months, and I wouldn't have to touch the five hundred grand Mount put in the checking account.

But what's the catch? With Mount, there's always a catch.

I flip through the pages of the contract, scanning quickly. It's a distribution agreement with all the standard terms and conditions that I'd normally expect to see.

When I turn to the last page, something catches my eye. Specifically, my name. The contract is contingent upon me being the point of contact through the duration of the distribution relationship, which is intended to renew annually with increasing quantities unless either party gives notice to terminate. The signature on it is a scribble I can't decipher.

I stride into the bedroom, but Mount's already gone.

"Damn you! I have questions!" I yell, but he obviously doesn't hear me.

I turn the door handle to the exit, expecting it to be locked. When it flies open with a yank, I almost fall on my ass. Mount's suited figure nears the corner at the end of the wide hallway.

"Hey! Our conversation is not over!"

His broad-shouldered form halts before slowly turning around to face me. He's at least thirty feet away, but I can see the expression on his face. There's no hint of the humor that was there when he handed me the box.

His long strides eat up the distance between us faster than I anticipate.

Oh shit. I swallow a lump in my throat and force myself to appear confident, even though I feel like a novice matador facing her first bull charge.

Maybe I should think before I yell at the scariest man in this city?

TWENTY-THREE

Mount

I WRAP MY HAND AROUND HER UPPER ARM, MY GRIP firm enough to get her attention, but not tight enough to cause pain or injury, as I rip the bedroom door open.

I can't remember the last time someone shouted at me like that, telling me we weren't finished.

Only she would dare.

It's on the tip of my tongue to tell her exactly that, but I remember Titan's words.

Check your ego at the door.

When I release Keira, she steps away with her spine straight, indicating the defiance I continually struggle to tame, but there's a hint of something else in her expression as she waits for me to speak. Dread.

I hate that look on her face. I no longer want her to fear me like everyone else. It doesn't bring me any satisfaction.

I close the door and lean against it, my arms

crossed over my chest. Her attention follows my every movement as though anticipating that I'll lash out in retaliation, and that realization banks the smoldering flames of my temper.

"Then by all means, let's continue it now."

Keira's fear shifts to confusion, which is fine with me. While I don't want her fear, I feel no guilt about keeping her off-balance. That means I have a chance to tip the scales in my favor.

She holds out the contract. "What is this?"

"I'm fairly certain you can read."

Her brow furrows in frustration. "You know that's not what I mean. Why would you give this to me?"

I swear, there has never been a more difficult woman to please. I keep my tone bored as I reply. "You'd rather not sell an extra six thousand cases a year? If that's true, I'm sure the buyer could find an alternate—"

Keira cuts me off. "Of course I want to, but who the hell is buying them? And how did you arrange it?"

The muscle in my jaw flexes as I rein in the urge to shut down her interrogation. *No one* questions me like this. And I don't know why the hell I let her.

The voice in my head calls bullshit. *You know exactly why.*

"The distributor caters to high-end liquor stores all over the country."

"I've never heard the name before, and I know all of the big ones."

"Not all of them, clearly."

"Do you own it?"

I debate whether to lie, but what's the point? "Yes."

A grimace graces her features. She's so frigging transparent with her facial expressions, and clearly not finished with her questions.

"Why would you do this? It doesn't make any sense. There have to be strings attached. I've figured that much out when it comes to you."

She's not wrong. In my world, nothing is freely given. Everything comes with a price.

I break it down for her. "For the duration of the contract, you work directly with me. Not your assistant or a salesman. *You*."

"So, it's not a gift. Because if it were, there would be no strings." She shakes the paper between us. "This is just another way for you to control me." Her voice is quiet, and her words hit me like a gut punch.

She's right. My first attempt to give her something I know she wants, and I fuck it up.

I snatch the contract out of her hand, pull a pen from my breast pocket, and take it over to the table. I scratch out the clause, initial it, and turn it back around.

"There." I shove the agreement at her.

The line between Keira's eyebrows deepens as her gaze darts between me and the document. "I don't understand."

My fingers crease the paper as my grip tightens on it. My jaw still tight, I reply with my final offer. "No strings and a healthy profit margin."

I'm giving up all the leverage in this deal and receiving nothing from her in return, which feels beyond foreign.

Keira's teeth tug her bottom lip into her mouth as

she reaches out to take the contract from me. Her every movement screams hesitation.

Because she doesn't fucking trust you, I remind myself.

"There has to be something else. You don't do anything that's not calculated, and you certainly aren't out to do me any favors."

I want to point out the fact that there's an extra five hundred grand in her checking account and her bank debts are paid, but I bite back the retort.

"Is it so hard to believe that I did it because it's a good deal for Seven Sinners, which means it's good for you?"

Her stubborn chin lifts another inch. "So, you're patronizing me?"

I count to ten, my temper flaring again. I swear, this woman lives to test me. I attempt to do something helpful and she throws it back in my face . . . *but only because I attached the golden handcuffs to it first.*

I release a breath, my temper ebbing once more. "No. I'm not patronizing you."

Keira gives me a short nod before gripping the contract tightly enough to crease the pages. Her chin stays high. "Then I'll let you know if I have any other revisions to request before I sign."

This woman . . . She has to learn that she can only push me so far before I will throw down the rules.

"This doesn't go to your lawyer. That's non-negotiable."

Mistrust flares in her gaze once more. She wants to fight me on that point, but manages to keep it in.

Finally, she nods. "Okay. But I'd be a shitty CEO if I didn't review it in detail before I sign, and that's not how I run my business."

Her statement knocks something loose in me, altering my perception of the woman standing before me. *Keira Kilgore, the CEO.* Not Keira Kilgore, the woman I plan to own.

Another piece of Titan's advice enters my mind. *Listen. Figure out what she wants. Give it to her.*

I can admit when someone else is right, and he nailed it.

The contract is a start, but I've got a long way to go.

TWENTY-FOUR

Keira

MY WORKDAY PASSES IN WHAT FEELS LIKE A matter of minutes. When I leave the office, Temperance is still on the phone finalizing details for the Voodoo Kings event, and I give her a wave. She smiles and makes a shooing motion out the door.

Scar is waiting at the curb per usual, and I slide into the backseat of the car. We've dispensed with all the hood nonsense after my escape, so when he starts driving in the opposite direction as I expect, I question him, even though I know he's not going to answer.

"Where are we going?"

His grunt of a response is all I get.

Thirty minutes later, we turn down the road to Lakefront Airport, and I'm even more confused.

"What's going on?"

Scar drives directly to a private hangar and parks near the front glass doors. He exits the car and opens my door, then leads me inside. I barely get a look at the posh lounge area that looks nothing like the molded plastic seating of a commercial airport before he pushes open another glass door and we step onto a red carpet runner leading across the tarmac to the stairs of a large, sleek private jet.

Whoa.

I take in the black-and-gold aircraft, and although I know nothing about planes, I'm willing to bet it's ridiculously expensive. There's no name or logo indicating who owns it, but I only need one guess.

Scar nods toward the stairs, and I hesitate for a moment.

To fly on the private jet or not? It isn't exactly a decision I thought I'd be making when I left Seven Sinners tonight. I can't lie and say I've never wondered what it would be like to fly in one . . . but the thought of the man either already inside or en route keeps my feet glued to the red carpet.

What's the worst that can happen? It's not like he hasn't kidnapped me already. The fact that this is my logic and rationalization is absolutely insane, but that's the impact Mount has had on my life.

The final thing that sways me is the contract from this morning. It was a gesture I still don't understand, but I couldn't find any more hidden traps in the legalese either.

Scar grunts from behind me, and I make my decision.

Screw it.

With measured steps, I cross the red carpet and

reach the plane. I balance my shoe on the first stair, grip the rails, and climb up into the cabin.

The interior matches everything else of Mount's—black, gold, and white.

Mount is seated in one of the plush black leather seats with a laptop open on the table in front of him. He looks up as I enter.

"What's going on?"

He closes the laptop and stands. "We're going out."

"Like on a date?" Disbelief hangs from every word.

Mount jerks a chin toward the leather seat across from his. "Sit. I'll tell the captain we're ready for takeoff."

I lower myself into the chair, trying to figure out what the hell his game is this time. First the contract this morning, and now this? *What's his angle?*

Mount returns momentarily, and the cabin seems to shrink now that the door is closed and we're locked inside. His presence does that to me all too often.

"Where are we going?" I ask, desperate to keep my mind off the fact that the aircraft begins to move.

I grip the arms of the seat, my knuckles turning white as the statistics about the crashes of private planes versus commercial flights run through my head. We taxi to the end of a runway, turn, and jerk into forward motion as the jet picks up speed.

Oh shit. What are my parents going to think when they find out I died with him?

The thought is ridiculous, but logic isn't exactly on my side right now. I'm nearly hyperventilating as the jet hurtles down the runway.

"Keira, look at me."

Mount's deep voice snaps me out of my panic, and I meet his gaze.

"What?"

When he unclips his seat belt, I want to yell at him to put it back on, but he moves to the chair beside me before I'm capable of forming the sentence.

"Are you afraid of flying?" he asks, and I'm too freaked out to appreciate the concern in his tone.

I shake my head rapidly. I know better than to admit weakness, especially to him.

"Then why do you look like you're going to throw up?"

I break his stare and look out the window. *Oh, sweet Jesus. We're almost off the ground. Bad idea.*

Mount reaches out to cup my cheek, bringing my gaze back to his. "Listen to me. You're fine."

"You don't know that."

"Yes, I do. Because I won't let anything happen to you."

I swallow at his admission, and my stomach flips. I'm not sure whether it's because of this latent fear of flying clawing through me, or because of Mount's penetrating stare. Maybe both.

I force myself to relax, muscle by muscle, until my spine curves into the leather cushion. "I forgot. You have a vested interest in making sure nothing does, because then who would pay the debt I owe?"

His thumb strokes my cheek, and I tense again at the uncharacteristic gesture.

"At some point, you're going to realize this is about far more than a simple debt." Mount's voice is low, but his words send my anxiety soaring.

"What do you mean?"

He finally releases his hold on my face and turns toward the empty seats opposite us, crossing an ankle over one knee. He doesn't look at me when he replies.

"You're smart. You'll figure it out eventually."

TWENTY-FIVE

Mount

DON'T HAVE ENOUGH FINGERS TO COUNT HOW MANY times Keira asks where we're going, and each time I refuse to tell her, her frustration grows.

When we hit the four-hour mark on the flight, her attitude spikes. "You better plan on getting me back on time for work tomorrow."

"I'm afraid that's not happening, but your assistant has been notified to expect your absence and cover for you."

"You told her? She can't know about this." Keira's tone is sheer panic. It's no surprise she doesn't want anyone to know of her connection to me, but the fact still irritates me.

"No. She received an email from you explaining."

Keira's eyes widen. "How? You better not have hacked my freaking email. That's just—"

"Easy?" I supply the correct adjective.

"You can't do that! Tell the pilot to turn the plane

around right now."

"The fact that you still think you can give me orders never ceases to amaze me."

Her temper rises, and fire burns in her gaze. "If you think taking me to some private island is going to somehow make me easier to control, you've completely misjudged me."

If I hadn't had that conversation with Lucas Titan, I might have thought of doing something like that, but his words made a sizeable impact.

"It is an island."

"You—"

Before Keira can unleash whatever expletives she's planning, I pull a file from beneath my laptop and drop it in her lap. She flips it open and stares down at it before jerking her shock-filled gaze up to mine.

"Oh my God," she whispers. "We're going to Dublin? To the Global Whiskey and Spirts Conference? Please tell me this isn't a joke, because it wouldn't be funny."

I raise an eyebrow. I'm not the joking type.

Keira's eyes look like they might bug out of her head. "Holy shit."

She drops the file that contains the doodled-on brochure I stole off her desk the first night I made myself at home in her office. She covers her face with both hands before bringing them together in a prayer-like position in front of her nose.

"I don't . . . I don't know what to say. This is . . . definitely not what I expected." She closes the file and continues to speak. "I've literally wanted to go to GWSC since I was old enough to know what it was."

I shrug, barely restraining my triumphant grin. "Well, now you're going."

"I don't know what to say."

Her gaze meets mine, and there's something in it I've never seen before. At least, not directed at me. A mix of awe, gratitude, and something else . . . *Joy*, I think.

"Then don't."

She shakes her head. "No. I have to." She pauses, pressing her lips together. "Thank you. I don't know why you're doing this, but . . . thank you."

TWENTY-SIX

Keira

I JERK AWAKE IN MOUNT'S ARMS AS HE SETTLES ME into the backseat of a car. "Where are we?"

"Dublin. You missed the rest of the flight. Also, you snore."

My mouth drops open. "I do not."

One corner of his mouth quirks upward. "You do at altitude and when you're drunk."

The driver closes the door and I shoot Mount a glare, but it's impossible to keep it in place as the car pulls away from an airport and onto the streets leading into Dublin.

Giddiness fills me. I've wanted to come here my whole life. This is the city and the country where my family comes from, where our whiskey was born. This is my heritage. My roots. I still can't believe the man beside me is the one who finally made it happen.

"I'm really here," I whisper as I stare out the window, taking in all the wonderful sights as we near the city. It's early morning, and the city is coming to life for the day.

"Where does your family come from in Ireland?" Mount asks.

"Here. Dublin."

"Then it makes sense why you've always wanted to come."

I nod, a lump rising in my throat. "The original distillery went out of business when the whiskey market crashed, and my great-grandfather brought his family over during Prohibition. They ended up in New Orleans, and he started making bootleg whiskey because no one would hire him to do anything else."

"It must be nice to know where you came from."

I tear my gaze from the window and look at him, but Mount has already turned away. I recall the story I've heard about him, that he was abandoned as a baby in front of a church. I've always wondered if it's true, and his statement makes me think it absolutely is.

"I googled you, you know." I never intended to admit it, but it slips out.

He shifts, locking his attention on me again. "And?"

"There was nothing. Nothing at all. How is that even possible?"

"Money. Power. My desire for privacy. Other peoples' fear."

"Have you ever turned that money and power in the direction of finding your roots?"

His expression turns dark. "No, and I never will."

"Why not?" I know I should leave it alone, and yet I can't help but ask the question.

"Because who gave birth to me doesn't have fuck-all to do with who I am or what I do."

I let the topic lapse and stare out the window again, soaking up Dublin as we turn onto narrow streets before crossing the River Liffey. But my excitement is dampened by Mount's answer.

I can't imagine what it must have felt like to be abandoned. To know that your parents didn't want you. My father always wanted a son and got three daughters instead, and it was bad enough knowing that growing up. But in comparison, my childhood was an absolute dream compared to Mount's.

For the first time, when I look at his profile, I don't see the devil in a suit who has the power to turn my body against me and mess with my head. Instead, I see a man who must have fought overwhelming odds to get to where he is today. I have no idea how he built the empire he rules, and I doubt the question would be well-received.

Who would have guessed that it only took one trans-Atlantic flight and a drive through the city I've dreamed of visiting my whole life to realize that Lachlan Mount isn't a myth or a legend. He's just a man. A dangerous one, certainly, but still just a man.

It changes nothing, I tell myself, but I'm not sure I believe it.

We reach the tall hotel with ornate Victorian architecture and are escorted immediately to a massive suite.

"Your luggage will be delivered directly, sir," the concierge tells him as Mount hands him a large bill.

He carries euros? Between the jet and the service, I'm beginning to realize that regardless of the city or country we're in, Mount's life is completely different from mine.

Another thought occurs to me. "I have luggage?" He already shocked me by having my passport.

"Of course. G assembled a wardrobe for you and had it delivered to the jet before you arrived. I was assured that you'll have everything you need, but if you don't, you can buy it here."

Mount's posture stiffens as though he's expecting an argument from me, but he's way off base.

"Are you kidding? I'm in *Dublin*, a city I've wanted to see since I was a kid, and for a conference where I could learn things and make connections that can take Seven Sinners to the next level. I'm not going to waste time being picky about clothes when there's so much to see and do. As long as he didn't pack only lingerie, I couldn't care less."

Mount eyes me like I've grown a second head. "You are nothing like any other woman I've ever met."

His expression turns unreadable, and I have no idea how to respond. Thankfully, a knock on the door puts a halt to that conversation.

After our luggage is delivered into the bedroom of the suite, the bellhop faces us. "Is there anything else you require, sir? We're at your service."

Mount turns to me. "What do you want to eat? You must be starving."

It's morning here, obviously, but to me it's still the middle of the night. "I don't know what meal we should be eating right now."

"Doesn't matter. Just tell me what you want."

It's on the tip of my tongue to say I don't care, that I'll have whatever he's having, but I stop myself. *Mount's giving me a choice.* From the beginning, he's offered so few of those, and this one stands out in stark relief.

"A Belgian waffle with butter and syrup, and a side of bacon."

The bellhop nods, and Mount adds his order.

"Steak and eggs. And send up a bottle of every Irish whiskey you stock in the hotel bar."

I give the bellhop credit, because he doesn't look nearly as surprised by this request as I must. Again, Mount slides a large bill into the man's hand before he leaves.

"What's with the whiskey?"

Mount shoots me a sideways glance. "Isn't that why we're here? To learn and network as much as you can?"

He actually listened.

"Yes."

"Then I figure a bottle of each of the whiskeys they have will help you start prepping all your questions for the CEOs of the competition."

"Like they'll even talk to me," I say with a laugh. "When I said make connections, I was thinking more along the lines of suppliers and buyers. Small ones. My level. I'm not exactly the CEO of a multinational con-glomerate yet. I'm still running a tiny operation that's barely profitable."

Mount closes the distance between us and stares down at me. "Don't, for a single second, put yourself in a category beneath anyone here. Walk into this conference like you're their equal, because you are. Your operation may be small now, but as you told me, you're not a shitty CEO and you're still just getting started. You want to rule the whiskey world? Then act like you already do."

His words resonate within me, giving me a boost of confidence I didn't realize I needed. "You don't exactly strike me as the pep-talk type."

His lips flatten. "I'm not."

That comment hits me even harder, because it means his little speech was unique for me. Warmth curls in the vicinity of my chest.

"Thank you. For all of this. It means a lot to me." I lift my lips to press a kiss to his square jaw, now dark with stubble. When I lower myself on my heels to back away, Mount snakes an arm around my waist, yanking me against his chest.

"So that's what it takes. A trip to Ireland. Duly noted."

I don't have time to process his statement before his lips crash down on mine, his tongue stealing inside and taking over.

When he lifts me off my feet, my legs wrap around his waist instinctively. He carries me into the bedroom, and we land on the bed with a hard bounce. Mount's weight presses against me as I bury my hands in his hair.

I tell myself it's gratitude fueling my actions, but I

refuse to look deeper.

Mount tears the blouse from my body, sending buttons flying. He has my skirt shoved up around my waist when a knock comes at the outer door of the suite.

"Shit. The food," I say on a harsh breath.

"Fuck the food."

"That works for me."

We both ignore the continued knocking, and the subsequent phone ringing, in favor of devouring each other.

For the first time, the power struggle doesn't take precedence. This is something different. Something . . . more daunting.

I push the disturbing thought away as Mount frees his cock and shoves my panties to the side, finding me already wet. He never breaks my stare as he pushes inside, slowly this time, burying himself inch by inch. When he's fully seated, he growls a single word in my ear.

"*Mine.*"

It's the scariest thing I've ever heard him say, because I'm starting to believe him.

TWENTY-SEVEN

Mount

KEIRA MISSED REGISTRATION. MOSTLY DUE TO THE fact that we fell asleep and I woke her up with my head between her legs, teasing her clit with her new jewelry.

I sent a request down to the hotel staff to retrieve any necessary information from registration, and that gave us a few more hours, during which I didn't let her out of bed. At least, not until both of us decided that food was imperative.

When Keira walks into the cocktail party that evening, I follow a half step behind her, using my height to survey the crowd for threats while keeping my face impassive. My little hellion took my words to heart and shows no hesitation or uncertainty, holding herself like a queen in this male-dominated room.

Heads swivel as she strolls through the crowd, and it doesn't have a damn thing to do with the designer dress she's wearing. She's magnetic. Vibrating with energy.

"They're all wondering who you are," I tell her as we order drinks at the bar. Whiskey neat for both of us, made by the company with the biggest share of the whiskey market.

"More like they're wondering who you are," she whispers.

"Care to make a wager?"

She rolls her eyes. "Not against you. I have a feeling you always win."

"You're finally catching on."

We turn and survey the room, each sipping our whiskey. I can't see into her head, but I'm willing to bet she's scanning for familiar faces and devising a plan of attack.

A smile attempts to quirk my mouth because I'm doing the same.

Thankfully, there's no one in this crowd I recognize—at least, not yet. There's no doubt my reach extends far beyond New Orleans, and while I have a large stake in the liquor distribution business, my CEO is the public face of the company. I only manage as necessary from behind the scenes. He's here somewhere, but if he values his position, he'll heed the warning I sent before we left that I'm not to be approached.

This week is an anomaly for me. I don't have to be Lachlan Mount, the man whose brutality inspires fear and respect. This week, I can be whoever the hell I want. There's a certain allure that anonymity presents, and I embrace it. As Keira engages with suppliers, distributors, and competitors, I step back, letting her take center stage. She transforms from the defiant, stubborn female I've been determined to bend to my will into an impressively shrewd and intelligent businesswoman.

This isn't a shock to me, by any means. I've been watching her for long enough to know this is the case, but I've never had the opportunity to see her in action, up close and personal.

As she mingles, each person she speaks with is captivated by her, and I'm nothing but an afterthought.

What does shock me, however, is how liberated I feel.

Back in our suite later, Keira splashes whiskey into two glasses and hands me one.

"Sláinte," she says, raising hers to clink against the rim of mine. I repeat the toast back to her as she lifts the tumbler to her lips, draining it in a single drink.

"No savoring?"

She shakes her head. "It's not as good as Seven Sinners. Not many are."

From anyone else, it would sound like a boast, but from Keira, it's a simple fact. She believes in her product down to her bones.

Maybe more than I've ever believed in anything.

She opens another bottle and pours a small measure into a new glass.

"It still amazes me that you can drink so much for someone your size."

Keira lifts this glass to her nose and sniffs. "Mother's milk, I guess. It's in my blood. I've been drinking whiskey nearly my whole life. God, if social services had a clue I was tasting at eight years old, I'm sure my parents would've been all over the news."

Her remark turns my thoughts to all my run-ins with social services, and then all the time I spent avoiding them. "I'm sure they had more pressing cases to worry about."

She nods, completely absorbed in tasting the whiskey, and misses the darker edge of my statement. She shoots a genuine smile at me, which does a better job chasing away the demons of my past than the entire fifth of liquor would.

"Thank you. Especially for tonight. I . . . I honestly didn't know what to expect." Sincere gratitude rings with each word.

"I didn't do anything."

She shakes her head. "That's just it. I honestly thought we would step into that room and you would take over. That I'd be the one standing in silence while you commanded their attention."

"That's not why we're here." It bothers me that she thinks I'd steal this experience from her, but what evidence have I given her to expect anything else from me?

Keira doesn't hesitate to call me on it. "I know, but that's who you are. I didn't think you were capable of *not* taking over." She pauses, her top teeth digging into her bottom lip before releasing it. "I misjudged you, and I'm not too proud to admit it."

I reach for a random bottle and splash another three fingers into my glass. "Don't start giving me credit for qualities I don't have." Her first impression of me is much closer to the truth. I toss the whiskey back as carelessly as she did. Maybe getting drunk tonight isn't a bad idea.

"Stop. Please. This is important to me, and I'm going to get it out whether you want to hear it or not."

I lower the glass to the bar with a nod and cross my arms over my chest to wait.

"You were different. This was different. I . . ." She trails off again for a beat. "I hate talking about him. Especially now." Her gaze drops to the floor.

When she says *him*, a rumble of possession roars through me. I spit his name out so she doesn't have to. "Hyde, you mean?"

She nods.

"What about him?" My tone sharpens with each word dealing with the subject of the man. I hold myself stiff, wondering what comparison she's going to make between us, knowing it can't possibly be in my favor.

"He had to be the center of attention, have the most say in any conversation. *I* was the one who grew up in that distillery like it was my second home, and he'd been there for all of five minutes before his ego was nearly too big to fit through the door. *I* was the CEO, but he marginalized me at every opportunity. We were supposed to be a team. That's what he promised me. But he didn't understand the first thing about teamwork."

My hands curl into fists. I wish I'd killed the fucker personally, because obviously he did more damage to her than I realized.

"Hyde was a low-level con, through and through.

You weren't equipped to see it coming."

"Maybe not, but I was dumb enough to fall for it," she says, blinking back tears.

Hoping Saxon made that piece of shit suffer, I hold up a hand to stop her. "You didn't stand a chance, and I'm not insulting you when I say that."

Keira turns away, lifting both hands to her face, and I imagine she's wiping away tears. Tears that motherfucker is still causing from the grave. This ends now.

I wrap a hand around her arm and turn her to face me. "Stop. He doesn't deserve another fucking second of your time, let alone another tear."

"I just feel so stupid. And then I'm barely free of him and you swoop in, probably because you realized I'm such a fucking idiot and an easy mark. I didn't stand a chance against you either, did I?"

I release her and drop my hands to my sides, consciously flexing my fingers out from the fists they instinctively curl into.

I lower my voice, but every word is perfectly clear. "Don't fucking compare me to that piece of shit. I am not Brett Hyde."

Another tear tips over her lid, and I can't stop myself from reaching out to cup the side of her face. She flinches as I touch her, and I hate causing that reaction. I swipe a thumb beneath her lid and catch the next one that falls.

"I don't need to overshadow you in your element. This is your world. I expect you to go out there and conquer it."

She sniffles and brushes away the remainder of the

tears—and my hand. She doesn't realize I never offer comfort, and having it rejected is a sharp jab into a raw spot I didn't know I had.

I step back, gripping the bar with both hands, and wait for her to lift her gaze back to mine. When she does, I tell her the absolute truth.

"And no, you didn't stand a chance against me. I always get what I want."

TWENTY-EIGHT

Keira

I DON'T KNOW IF MOUNT'S LAST STATEMENT IS meant to rile me up, but that's exactly what it does. I offered him honesty, and he responded with dominance. Like always.

So I'll give him what he expects from me. Attitude.

"And what do you want right now, *Mount*?" I stress his name because, for a moment, he seemed like a man I could confide in, and now he's the arrogant bastard I've faced since the beginning.

"What I've wanted since the beginning. *You.*"

His hand moves at lightning speed, snatching mine and pulling me against him. I can't miss the hard bulge shielded by the thin material of his suit pants as he turns me in a circle.

"So, this whole act tonight was just to get me into bed?" I look up at him in defiance and watch his eyes narrow and his expression darken.

"I don't need an act for that. You've already agreed

to all my terms. Whenever I want, and willing."

My jaw clenches at his reminder. "Do they teach classes for that kind of arrogance, or were you born with it?"

All softness I felt toward him melts away like snow in the bayou, and it feels like we're back to square one. *Except I'm in Dublin. And he brought me here.*

Facing this man is like taking on a Category 5 hurricane. My conflicting emotions surge within me.

Mount's laugh is low and harsh. "You think I'm arrogant now? You've barely scratched the surface. For the record, just because I let you take the lead in your world doesn't mean you get to call the shots anywhere else."

"You're impossible." I hiss the words, but my body is already responding to his, and it's taking all my self-control not to rub up against him like an animal in heat. Every bit of pressure heightens the sensation, thanks to my piercing.

"Pot, meet kettle," he says.

"Fuck your pot and kettle."

"All I want to fuck is you." His gaze burns over my skin, and his nostrils flare as his free hand wraps around the back of my thigh, dragging upward until his palm skates under the fabric of my dress to grip my ass. "And you want it just as bad."

"Not tonight."

He lowers his lips close to my ear, and whispers a single word. "Liar."

I have two options—murder him in this gorgeous hotel suite and spend the rest of my life on the run, or give in to the insanity and climb him like my body is dying for me to do.

"I still hate you."

His teeth close over my earlobe. "No, you don't. You just hate that you want me as badly as I want you." He tugs and my nipples harden into points. "Admit it, and I'll give you what you want."

"This isn't a new game. We both know you can make me want you, and it won't mean anything except that you know how to play the game better than I do."

He releases his hold on me completely. Surprised, I stumble back on my heels, catching myself on the bar.

Mount takes a step backward and shrugs off his jacket, leaving it folded over the back of the living room sofa. With another step back, he loosens the knot of his tie and tosses it on a chair. One more step, and the top two buttons of his shirt are undone, revealing the tanned, thick column of his neck. Another step, and the remaining buttons are undone and his shirt falls open, revealing his hard chest and rippling abs.

He stands in the middle of the suite, tucking his hands into his pockets as he meets my gaze. "I want to hear it now. Before I drag you to the brink and you're willing to say anything for me to let you come."

I lick my lips and flatten them. My inner muscles are already clenching, wetness soaking my thong as my body anticipates what's coming next.

Murder or pleasure. What happened to my life that these two choices became equally viable outcomes to the same issue?

Mount happened.

"Fine. I'll admit it. You win."

Mount shakes his head slowly. "This isn't about winning. This is about making it crystal fucking clear in your head that you crave what I give you. You don't just want me to take control—*you need it*."

He's right. There's no way I can deny it. We both know I'm a shitty liar.

"Then take it," I tell him.

Again, his ridiculously handsome face moves slowly from side to side. "No, tonight you're going to give it to me willingly."

"What do you mean?"

He tips his head toward the floor-to-ceiling windows, hidden by opulent window treatments. "Open the curtains."

My brain spins at his order. *Where is he going with this?*

"Why?"

"Ask another question, and I swear you won't come tonight."

I bite down on my lip because my natural instinct is to question his every order. But the idea of being denied orgasms all night, while he undoubtedly can give me many, isn't something I want to contemplate.

His dark eyes flare with heat as I step toward the drapes and yank them wide open. The lights in the room are low, but still bright enough to give a clear view inside.

"Hands at your sides. Don't move."

In the reflection of the glass, I watch as Mount unbuttons his cuffs, strips off his shirt, and drops it on the floor before stalking toward me.

The cold from the window is already sending chills through my body, and Mount's heat at my back creates warring sensations that are normal when I'm dealing with him.

The zipper on my dress hisses as Mount slides it down. His fingers push the straps off my shoulders, but I catch them with my elbows, holding the dress against my chest.

"Someone could see."

His voice is low but implacable. "They can look, but they can't fucking touch what's mine."

Of their own volition, my arms drop to my sides and my dress slides down, puddling at my feet.

"Step out of it."

Mount's teeth graze my shoulder before he drags them up the column of my neck, and I hold in a moan.

"Are you going to make me repeat myself?" He growls it in my ear, nipping my lobe.

This is the power struggle. The one I crave. When he said I wanted this, he wasn't wrong.

"No."

I comply, and Mount kicks the expensive designer dress aside before closing a hand around my wrists, lifting my hands to press them both palm-first against the window. I shiver, my nipples pebbling against the lace of my strapless bra as he growls in my ear.

"Keep your hands on the window or your punishment will come later, and I promise it won't be nearly as enjoyable as this."

I nod, and Mount releases his hold. I stay in

position as his fingers skim down my arms to my shoulders before circling my rib cage to thumb my nipples through my bra.

"I don't spend nearly enough time on these gorgeous tits." He releases the clasp of my bra, sending it to the floor, and my breasts spill into his hands. He toys with my nipples, sending jolts of pleasure straight to my center.

My moan slips free, and it urges him on. "Bend forward. Put them on the window. Get them nice and cold. I want them even harder for me."

Even though my instinct is to balk at how obscene his order is, I follow his command, sucking in a breath when my sensitive skin touches the chilled glass.

"Good girl," Mount says, right before his palm connects with my ass with a smack.

I straighten, but he grips my hips to pull me back into position as he grinds the hard length of his erection against me.

"You worried about them seeing you now?"

"I don't know," I whisper.

His hand slides around to my stomach and skims down to toy with the waistband of my thong, snapping the thin material before it falls away. He cups my center with his palm, his teeth grazing my other shoulder as he growls in satisfaction.

"Then I better show everyone out there who owns this pussy, in case they get any ideas."

The forbidden thrill of being watched only adds to my confused emotions. Mount slips one finger between my lips, already finding me wet. When he drags it around my piercing, my hips move, my body desperate for more contact.

"You gonna tell me that I don't own this perfect cunt?"

His growled words make me even more frantic.

"No!" This time the word comes out on a harsh moan as he pushes two fingers knuckle-deep inside me.

"I didn't think so."

He fucks me deeper with his fingers, and my hands squeeze into fists. But I manage to keep them on the window, never breaking contact, not even when Mount frees his cock and works it between the cheeks of my ass.

"Someday soon, there won't be any question about who owns this ass either, because when I sink my cock inside it, you'll be screaming my name."

His filthy words trigger another drawn-out moan. Mount shifts, fitting the head of his shaft against my entrance, pushing forward just enough to nudge the tip inside.

I open my mouth, ready to beg, except this time he doesn't make me wait. He buries himself to the hilt in a single thrust. With both his hands pressing against mine on the glass, he powers into me without mercy, and I love every single second of it.

When I come, it's with a scream that all of Dublin must be able to hear—and see.

But in the circle of Mount's arms, I forget to care.

TWENTY-NINE

Mount

AFTER TWO DAYS OF PANEL DISCUSSIONS, I'VE learned more about whiskey and spirits than I ever wanted to know, but I have to admit I now have a stronger fascination with it. Plenty of what I've learned will go into practice to streamline my own business. Keira and I parted ways to cover more ground because she couldn't be in every presentation she wanted to hear.

Do I like letting her out of my sight into a crowd of men who stare at her like she's their next meal? Not particularly, but I also realize something equally as important that makes me want to kill them less—Keira doesn't see them. Not as men. She sees them as sources of knowledge, competitors, possible sales or potential suppliers.

She's one hundred percent business during the day, but as soon as we make it to the suite at night, everything changes. The power struggle continues, but she's bending more each time. Sometimes, it's all I can do not to drag her away from whatever vendor party we attend in the evening and fuck her in the elevator on the way up.

Only one thing holds me back—I won't take the risk of damaging the reputation and credibility she's building here. To Keira, that would be the ultimate unforgiveable sin. Against the window was different. I didn't tell her until afterward that it was tinted and no one could see us. Her furious glare was worth hearing her scream echo through the room when she came after we fought about it.

Like an addict craving his next fix, every time I'm with her, I'm chasing the same high. Except the difference between Keira and drugs? Every time with her gets *better*.

Today is the only free day of the conference. Tomorrow, we go back to panels during the day, and then a final gala with an award ceremony in the evening.

I would prefer to keep her in bed with my cock buried inside her all day, but I already made plans for us. I'm cursing them as she pulls on jeans and a form-fitting sweater, and slips a leather jacket over it.

Goddammit, she's fucking sexy. Naked. Clothed. In lingerie. It doesn't matter.

First step of addiction: admitting you have a problem.

Fuck that nonsense. I'm doing just fine.

THIRTY

Keira

AS A PRIVATE CAR CARRIES US THROUGH THE streets of Dublin, my excitement grows with every moment. I've barely been out of the hotel since we got here, but today, I finally get to see the city I've explored many times in my imagination.

"Where are we going?" I ask the silent man beside me.

"You'll see."

I roll my eyes, knowing that continually pushing for an answer isn't going to get me one. More likely than not, it'll end up with me getting my ass spanked and hating to admit that I liked it.

I keep quiet, soaking up the atmosphere of the city. The buildings are all so close together, reminding me of New Orleans, but are built with a different architectural style—some Georgian, some Victorian, and I'm not even sure what else. The sky is gray, but that doesn't stop people from filling the sidewalks, and tourists from climbing onto the green and red double-decker buses that make a circuit around the city.

I could only imagine what Mount would say if I tried to get him to ride on a bus. A soft laugh escapes me at the ridiculous idea.

"What?" he asks, and I turn away from the window to find his attention on me.

"I was trying to picture you riding one of those tourist buses."

"And you found that funny?"

"I found it ridiculous for me to try to picture, actually."

I turn my attention back out the window as the driver maneuvers through the narrow streets. A tall church comes into view, and it dawns on me what it is.

"That's Saint Patrick's Cathedral, isn't it?"

"I believe you're right. Padraig?"

Padraig, our driver for the day, chimes in. "Yes, ma'am. It's over eight hundred years old. Saint Patrick himself baptized people on those very grounds. Construction on the current building didn't start until about 1220."

The tall gray spires reach into the sky. The idea that Saint Patrick himself stood on that land, the man for whom my grandfather was named, fills me with an incredible sense of history.

We turn another corner, and on the right, long reddish-brown brick buildings stretch along the street. I realize they must be townhomes, but each one seems to have a different-colored door—red, white, green, yellow, blue, purple, or turquoise. A veritable rainbow.

"What's with the doors?"

The driver glances up in the rearview for a moment before explaining. "The townhouses all looked the same and were required to be uniform, but the residents started painting the doors different colors so they'd know which one was theirs. That way, your drunk neighbor didn't try to bash into your house after too many pints at the pub."

I laugh at his explanation, because it actually makes perfect sense. We turn another corner and then another, and I'm trying to soak it all in as the car slows to a halt in front of a large building with a name and a logo I know well. I've followed this family for the last couple of years. They have a history similar to my family's, and they inspired me when they undertook a massive building project. If I could bring Seven Sinners up to their level, I'll have achieved a huge chunk of the goals I've set for myself.

I jerk my gaze away from the golden phoenix logo on the gigantic building to look at Mount. "How did you know I wanted to come here?"

"Despite what you might think, I do pay attention."

I've spent at least half the conference trying to find a way to speak with the owner of this distillery, but I've never been able to catch him.

I blink, shocked that Mount noticed.

The driver parks and climbs out of the car before opening the door to let me out first. Mount follows me. The brisk Irish wind makes me grateful for the leather jacket, jeans, and sweater that G packed, but if there's a chance the owner's inside, I'd prefer to be wearing a suit or something more formal.

But there's no way. He must be in meetings all day like almost everyone else, even though this is our "free" day. I've been rebuffed in my attempts to set up a few meetings with CEOs of companies that are household names around the world, and hoped Mount didn't notice. Judging by this surprise, I'm betting he did.

"Enjoy your tour. I'll be waiting for your summons whenever you're ready," Padraig says as he closes the car door.

His words remind me that this distillery does exactly what Temperance and Jeff Doon want Seven Sinners to do—open its doors to the public for daily tours.

When we walk inside, the interior reminds me of my Seven Sinners remodel, and I'm making mental notes as Mount gives the woman behind the front counter my name.

"Of course. I'll let your guide know you've arrived. Shall I take your coats? It will be quite warm inside."

I hand mine off to her, as does Mount. He traded in his suit today for dark jeans, but I haven't seen what is under his jacket until this moment—a worn gray T-shirt with a Seven Sinners logo. It's been *years* since that T-shirt was made. My father was still running the company, and I was climbing my way up from the bottom rung of the ladder. The logo wear experiment lasted all of one year before Dad considered it a failure.

"Where did you get that?"

Mount gives me a sideways look. "Does it matter?"

"Yes."

He shrugs. "I've known about Seven Sinners a long time. Even before I knew about you."

My brain slips into overdrive as I try to figure out what that means, but our tour guide meets us at the entrance. It's none other than the CEO himself.

"Ms. Kilgore, it's a pleasure to meet you. I've heard we have some fierce competition coming out of New Orleans thanks to you and Seven Sinners." He shakes my hand with respect, and I remember what Mount told me.

Don't, for a single second, put yourself in a category beneath anyone here.

I guess this is where I employ the *fake it till you make it* approach.

"Mr. Sullivan, it's an honor. This is—" I turn to introduce Mount, but the CEO of Sullivan Distillery beats me to it.

"A man who needs no introduction." Deegan Sullivan holds out a hand to Mount, and the man beside me shakes it. "It's been a while, Mount. I'm assuming you got my case of whiskey as a thank-you?"

Mount nods, and my gaze darts between the two men like they're playing table tennis.

Mount knows Deegan Sullivan? Why am I even surprised?

"I did."

Deegan looks down at Mount's T-shirt. "But it seems your whiskey tastes have changed. I'm not sure you'll be impressed by what we have to offer at our tasting today."

Mount holds both hands palms up at his sides with

a twitch of a grin. "I'm NOLA born and bred. It isn't a stretch to figure where my loyalties lie. Either way, this visit isn't about me. Ms. Kilgore is ready for her tour, so I hope you're on your game, Deegan."

"Of course. It's Keira, right? I insist we dispense with the formalities."

"Yes, Keira. And that's fine. I have to admit I've been following your progress for a few years."

"And I yours. Making whiskey in the Irish tradition in New Orleans is certainly a way to catch people's attention."

"Some people's, I suppose."

"Would you like to see the distillery? We don't have any other tours for several hours, so we've got the place to ourselves."

"Absolutely," I reply as excitement bubbles up inside me.

"Since you're already a bit of an expert, I'll spare you the full lecture and we'll head right for the good stuff."

When Deegan pushes open a large door, the heat from the stills instantly hits me in the face, reminding me of Seven Sinners. We climb a flight of stairs to a metal catwalk that gives us a view of the whole operation in a single room. At Seven Sinners, due to the age of the distillery building, ours isn't so well organized.

"We get several deliveries a week of grain, and malted and unmalted barley, and we use special conveyers to transport it from the silos to the wet mill."

"Isn't that more normal for a brewing operation than a distilling operation?" I ask, mainly because I've been toying with the idea myself. But when I brought it up to my father last year, he dismissed it immediately.

"We're all about efficiency, and we find that works much better."

I walk to the edge of the platform, leaning over the railing to study the mill more closely. "I appreciate efficiency as well, but my father . . ." I trail off and find Deegan nodding as I glance back at him.

"Sometimes when you take the reins, you have to quit listening to what the older generation has to say. When the only answer they give you is *because it's tradition*, I'm of the opinion that technology probably has a better solution."

I've gone against my father's opinions several times, the first time with the massive bank loan and remodel. Changing the guts of the operation—other than switching to organic grain—is something I've never considered. But, apparently, I should.

Deegan moves to the next stage of the process. "I'm sure you recognize mash when you see it and smell it."

I inhale the familiar scent and ask a few questions about their temperature and timing, and Deegan is surprisingly open with his answers.

"I don't need to explain to you that the liquid is separated so we can send the wort into the fermenters, and the spent grain is used for animal feed."

I smile. "Yeah, I do have the basics down."

"More than, I'm sure."

As we move along the tour, talking about fermenting and the advantages of using both stainless and wooden casks, Mount stays a half step behind me, silent the entire time.

He's either bored out of his mind . . . or he's letting me take the lead, just like he did during the conference. For the first time, I give him the benefit of the doubt and think it's the latter.

The warmth that moves through me has nothing to do with the heat coming off the gorgeous copper pot stills, and everything to do with the man following me.

THIRTY-ONE

Mount

DIDN'T KNOW POT-STILL ENVY WAS A THING, BUT the way Keira gazes with longing at the three massive Italian-made stills tells me that it absolutely is.

"Seven Sinners uses triple distillation as well, doesn't it?" Sullivan asks, and Keira nods.

"That's the only process my family has ever used. Our motto is *make less, but make it the best*."

"And the strongest," Sullivan adds with a laugh. "We understand that here."

The two of them go back and forth with questions and answers until I'm certain Keira has soaked up enough information that she could go home and re-vamp Seven Sinners' entire process. The discussion of the myriad array of barrels used, maturation, vatting, and bottling would normally be something that I'd find somewhat interesting, but Keira's rapt attention makes it seem riveting.

At the end of the tour, nearly three hours later,

Sullivan shows us into the tasting room where there's a bar and gift shop.

Keira surveys the entire layout, envy rolling off her in waves.

"My assistant, Temperance, would be shoving this in my face right now, telling me *I told you so*." When both Sullivan and I look at her, she explains. "She's been after me to do exactly this for a long time. Bring people in, teach them what we do and why we do it so they feel a personal bond with the brand. Have them taste it and love it, and then sell them all the gear we can before they go on their way. Do you mind if I take some pictures?"

"Go right ahead. And you've basically hit it in a nutshell. That's exactly what we do," Sullivan says. "We're not Jack Daniel's or Jameson, a bottle that people might pick off the shelf because they've heard the name. But once someone has been through this distillery tour, they'll remember Sullivan whiskey for life, and hopefully buy it forever. It's the personal connection. That's why, when we built this facility, it was constructed with tours in mind."

Keira sighs. "I just did a massive renovation to bring us into the twenty-first century—late to the game, as always. We added a restaurant and gave the whole building a face-lift, but starting over and building a facility to cater to tours would be impossible. Not to mention the fact that we'd need to upgrade our equipment too."

"Maybe right now isn't the time, but you haven't been at the helm all that long, have you? You still have plenty of years to get to where you want to go."

"With unlimited funds, maybe . . . I'll just have to make the small changes I can, but keep the quality. I have room for a gift shop. We have the restaurant. I just have a feeling my lawyers would freak if I mentioned tours."

Sullivan grins. "Fuck the lawyers. All they want to do is get in the way. Find a way to make it happen. We're one of a kind here in Dublin. Sure, you can go tour the old Jameson building, but there's no whiskey being made there. You get a museum. That's great for people who recognize the name already, but if you want to stand out in someone's head, you need more."

As we sit down at one of the tables and sample flights of whiskey, Keira's mind is only halfway on the flavors Sullivan is describing. She's already working through his comments in her head.

And so am I.

THIRTY-TWO

Keira

WHEN WE WALK OUT OF THE SULLIVAN distillery, my brain is going a million miles an hour. Mount must have texted Padraig, because the driver pulls up and takes the case of whiskey that Deegan insisted we needed out of Mount's hands and stows it in the trunk.

I pull out my phone and make a dozen notes to myself about things to discuss with Temperance and Louis when I get back. I have plans. All the plans.

"Would you like me to take you back to the hotel, sir?" Padraig asks.

"That depends," Mount says, and I tear my attention from my phone and look up to meet his gaze. "What else can't you live without seeing in Dublin this time?"

This time. That makes it sound like I'll be coming back, and I decide right then that Mount's right. I *will* be back. But for now . . . I know exactly what else I want to see.

"I don't like beer that much, but I've always wanted to see Saint James's Gate and drink a pint at the Gravity Bar at the top of the Guinness Storehouse."

"Shall we head that way, then?" Padraig asks. "It's not far, still in the Liberties, and you can do a largely self-guided tour. It's a tourist favorite."

I want to say yes. I can't imagine Mount mingling amongst a crowd of people snapping pictures, but photos I've seen of the Gravity Bar were part of the inspiration for the restaurant on the top floor of Seven Sinners. Being this close to it and not going to see it would suck.

"Whatever the lady wants," Mount says, shocking the hell out of me. "Let's go to the Storehouse. If we're going to be tourists for a day, we might as well do it right."

Ten minutes later, we're exiting the car onto a cobblestone street next to a massive stone-and-brick building. I head for the door that reads WELCOME TO THE HOME OF GUINNESS. Inside, it's a complete madhouse. The noise of hundreds of tourists echoes upward through the open center. Mount's hand never leaves the small of my back as we stand in line to purchase tickets, and then wander through the gift-shop area to the escalator to start the tour.

"Arthur Guinness was a smart man."

Mount nods to a sign painted on what looks like a partial replica of a fermentation tank. It reads:

NOT EVERYTHING IN BLACK AND WHITE MAKES SENSE.

The fact that Mount noticed the sign makes me think of the overwhelming presence of black, white, and gold in the two suites I've seen in his compound. And the dining room. And the hallways.

"Did you get your decorating tips from Guinness?" When I turn to face him, he's on the step below me, putting us at eye level.

Mount's laugh booms out, echoing over the chatter, which I swear goes quiet for a moment. "No. No, I did not."

"Then what's that all about?"

The humor in his expression fades, and I don't think he'll reply, but he does.

"It's a reminder."

"Of what?"

"That there is such a thing as absolutes. Good and evil. Right and wrong."

That explains the black and white. "But what's with the gold?"

"The golden rule. He who has the most gold makes the rules . . . and gets to determine where those lines between right and wrong are drawn."

I feel like Mount just gave me a peek inside his head, and I'm not sure what to do with that information. In this situation, undoubtedly, Mount has the most gold, therefore he makes the rules. But right and wrong, good and evil . . . those concepts don't seem like they'd trouble him much. Or, if anything, I'd assume he'd say he lives in the shades of gray.

Mount lifts his chin and glances up. "You're missing the good stuff."

I look where he indicated. It's a glass sign that reads:

This is the storehouse where, for almost a century
the magic process of fermentation took place.
Construction began in July 1902. Four years later,
fermentation began and continued until 1988.

My curiosity about the black, white, and gold is pushed aside for a moment as the history of where I'm standing washes over me. It might not have a damn thing to do with whiskey, which is my passion, but my roots and their ties to the city feel stronger than ever.

Mount and I wander up each floor, reading the placards and listening to the holograms describe the history of Guinness. What impresses Mount the most is that Arthur Guinness had the foresight and confidence to sign a nine-thousand-year lease for the storehouse property.

"That took balls. Have to respect the man for that, if nothing else."

"It was crazy! They must have thought he was insane," I say.

Mount shakes his head. "Brilliant, more likely."

After learning about how to properly build a pint and tasting a sample, we finally make it to the Gravity Bar, and I'm able to see the famous 360-degree view of Dublin beyond the glass. It's surreal.

Mount positions himself behind me. He places his hands on either side of mine, resting on the tall table with the remains of our pints between us, protecting me from the jostling of the massive number of people crammed into the space.

"I can't believe I'm actually here." I turn my head to meet his gaze. "Thank you. I know this isn't what you would've picked to do today, but it meant a lot to me."

He doesn't answer but his dark gaze pierces mine, making me wish I had another peek into this man's head. He's an enigma.

Mount's palm slides against the small of my back once more before he replies. "Finish your pint. We're not done with Dublin yet."

THIRTY-THREE

Mount

I WANT HER TO KISS ME. RIGHT THERE IN THE BAR, I want her to turn around and fucking kiss me of her own free will. When she doesn't, I force down my disappointment and lead her down the stairs and out of the building, telling myself that at least she'll never think of Guinness without remembering this trip. *And me.*

When we drive past the famous Saint James's Gate as we leave the Liberties, Keira reaches over and grabs my arm.

"There it is! That's it."

It's the shiny black-lacquered gate with the golden harp and Guinness name beneath it that I've seen in many an ad for the company, but Keira doesn't care. She's practically bouncing in her seat at experiencing it for herself, and her excitement is contagious.

I've been to Dublin before. It wasn't pleasant business, but it had to be done. I couldn't tell you a thing about the city after I left except it was gray and rainy, and the river looked an unhealthy shade of green.

But now I'm seeing it all through Keira's eyes, and it's a completely different perspective. She's successfully changed my opinion of Dublin, solely by experiencing it with her at my side.

When she asks Padraig to drop us off at a true Irish pub near Temple Bar, I don't argue. I let her pull me out of the car when he stops in front of a restaurant that fits the bill, and lead me inside.

The food is greasy, but filling, which apparently is exactly what we need, because Keira gets it in her head that she wants to see as many of the pubs in Temple Bar as possible. If I were to compare it to New Orleans, I'd describe Temple Bar as the French Quarter of Dublin, which is probably why we both feel so at home here. The buildings are all connected, and we wander the uneven cobblestone streets with no particular destination in mind but wherever Keira's fancy takes us.

In between pubs, she drags me into brightly colored shops and buys the most random things. My favorite? An inexpensive but creative necklace.

"I think it suits me. Don't you?" She's tipsy from drinking all day—whiskey, beer, and cider, the combination of which has stripped her of her normal stiffness around me.

I offer up the euros to pay for the necklace and lift it out of her palm. It's a hand flipping the bird, and the knuckles are tattooed with two words: WORK HARD. My lips twitch with the urge to smile as I fasten it around her neck.

"It definitely suits you."

"But not tonight. Tonight is for fun only. Nothing else." As though punctuating her slightly slurred words, she pulls the tie that has kept her hair in a low pony-tail all day and shakes out her red mane. "I let my hair down. Now it's your turn."

The proprietor looks thankful when we step out of the shop, because he's on the verge of closing. The sun has gone down, and Irish pub music spills out into the streets.

Keira leans into me. "So?"

I'm not clear on how tipsy she is, but she's missing an important piece of the puzzle. "I can't let my hair down." I shove a hand through it. "It's not long enough."

"Then you have to do something else."

"What?" Again, the corners of my mouth tug upward.

"That." She points to my face. "Smile. You hardly ever smile. You always look so . . . stern."

When she makes an attempt to mimic my normal expression, a laugh breaks free from my throat.

"Yes!" Her face lights up in satisfaction.

"Is that all you want from me?"

She shakes her head as we reach the door to an-other pub. "No. Tonight, let's pretend you're not Mount and I'm not your payment on a debt. Let's just be Lachlan and Keira. Can we do that?"

It's on the tip of my tongue to tell her she's a hell of a lot more than that, but I hold it back. Instead, I make a request of my own.

"On one condition."

We step into the bar, and the musician onstage has the entire place packed.

"What?" Keira has to yell over the crowd for me to hear her, so I wrap both arms around her waist and lift her off her feet so my mouth is level with her ear.

"Say my name again."

"Come on, lads and lasses. Let's get ta dancin," the man onstage cries out, urging people toward the dance floor.

Keira bites her lip, and the craving to kiss her hits me hard again. She places both hands on my shoulders and leans in.

My breath stops for an instant, expecting her lips to hit mine, but they bypass my mouth for my ear.

"Dance with me, Lachlan. Dance with me in Dublin."

THIRTY-FOUR

Mount

KEIRA PASSES OUT IN MY ARMS ALMOST AS SOON AS the car door closes and Padraig drives us back to the hotel.

I've gambled and won fortunes time and again, amassed money until it no longer has any meaning except for the power it allows me to wield. I've built a goddamned empire. But none of those things can give me what I want right now.

"Dance with me, Lachlan."

Her request was ludicrous. I don't dance, but in that pub, with the Irishman and his guitar encouraging everyone to join in, I gave her what she wanted.

For one night, I've gotten the chance to be someone else. Anyone but me. And that man was able to sweep this woman off her feet, literally and figuratively.

Keira sighs, curling into my body.

It's too bad she probably won't remember any of it.

Or maybe it's better that way. Unlike me, she won't spend the rest of her life wishing for another night like this.

THIRTY-FIVE

Keira

WHEN I WAKE, MY HEAD POUNDS LIKE AN ENTIRE troop of Irish step dancers is using it as a stage for a performance. I roll over in bed, naked but for the sheet and down comforter covering me, and no memory of how I got there or managed to get my clothes off.

I glance at the clock to find it's almost one in the afternoon.

"Shit." I've missed all the morning panels. They weren't nearly as important as the ones earlier in the week, probably because so many people duck out before the last day, but still. This is my first conference, and I planned to make the most of it.

I sit up in bed and haul the covers off. A note flutters to the floor as though it was lying next to me. When I reach down to grab it, everything I've consumed in the last day feels like it's about to come up.

I'm officially too old for whatever the hell happened

last night.

I've never been the type to get blackout drunk because my tolerance is higher than most people's, and yet my memories from last night are fractured, at best.

I remember the distillery. Guinness. Eating. Wandering Temple Bar and hitting a few pubs. But beyond that, it gets grainy.

When my stomach steadies, I reach down for the note.

There's hot coffee in the living room. Drugs on the nightstand for your head.
Drink some water. Shower and call down for food.
Your stylists arrive at five.

There's no signature, but I recognize the bold scrawl.

The last part confuses me. *Stylists?*

Then I remember the last evening of the conference is tonight—the gala and the award ceremony for the whiskey-and-spirit-tasting contest that's been going on all week. I haven't thought much about it since Seven Sinners didn't enter because I wasn't planning to come.

The way I feel right now, I'm not sure I'll feel human by then, but I stand and find my balance. I can hear his authoritative tone ordering me to comply with the rest of his instructions, and even though it's second nature to rebel, I don't intend to.

My stomach has other plans, however, and I bolt for the bathroom.

Ugh.

After I finish heaving up my guts, I rinse my mouth, brush my teeth, and drink some water so I can take the ibuprofen on the nightstand. Coffee is too much for me right now. When my stomach stops flopping, I head for the shower.

Food can come later, because it sounds like a horrible plan right now.

After spending what feels like a year under the hot spray, I force myself to turn off the water and step out.

"Here."

I screech as Lachlan holds out a fluffy white bath sheet.

Lachlan? When the hell did he become Lachlan?

I grab the towel and wrap it around my body, feeling more naked than ever before, regardless of the fact that he's already seen everything I have to offer.

"Did you order food?"

"Not yet."

"Good. I called down for room service."

Still reeling from the massive shift in my head, I don't ask what he ordered. "What happened last night?"

I expect to see an arrogant grin cross his face, or perhaps a forbidding scowl, but he remains expressionless.

"You had a little more to drink than either of us realized."

I tug the towel tighter, tucking the tail between my breasts before meeting his gaze. "You know that's not what I mean."

"Does it matter if you don't remember?"

I pinch my lips together, wanting to demand de-tails, but I already know he won't give them to me. "I think you're more stubborn than I am, you know?"

That gets a reaction out of him. A single quirk of one corner of his mouth. "By a slim margin."

"You're not going to tell me anything?"

A knock sounds on the outer door of the suite and he turns, ignoring my question.

"I'll get the door. You're going to eat."

THIRTY-SIX

Mount

FOR THE LAST TWO HOURS, I'VE BEEN BOOTED FROM our room while the stylists I hired to do Keira's hair and makeup work their magic. I saw to it that she ate, slept some more, and was ready and appeared relatively human when they arrived.

I'm in the hotel bar when I get a call from J on my secure line.

"We've got a problem."

"What?" I reach for my wallet, tossing some cash on the bar before making my way to one of the sound-proof booths available for calls.

"Cartel is asking around about the disappearance of their lieutenant."

"You've gotta be shitting me." I locate a free booth close to the door behind me.

"No, and they're getting insistent about it."

I think back to that night and the several witnesses in the room. The crooked city councilman, the hypocritical megachurch preacher skimming from the donations, and the oil baron with an ego bigger than mine.

All of whom I have information on, and all of whom would love for the cartel to take me out in hopes that their secrets would die with me.

"Everyone knows the consequences if they talk. Feel free to send reminders on my behalf."

J knows that by *reminders*, I mean a team of enforcers.

"I think the preacher is the weak link. He's a pussy," J says.

"No. He's the least of our worries. He doesn't want to give up his Gulfstream or his mistress. We've got the least amount of leverage on the oilman. Watch him. If the cartel goes to question him, make sure he's temporarily unavailable."

"How temporarily?"

"Let him know that it'd be in his best interest to take his family on an extended vacation to their villa in Italy."

"And if he balks?"

"Just fucking do it, J. You want to prove you can handle more? Handle this shit."

J's tone changes. "It's under control. Enjoy the rest of your vacation."

"You run into problems, call me. No surprises."

"Got it, boss."

I hang up, annoyed that this escape of a vacation has been interrupted by cartel bullshit.

J knows as well as I do that the cartel will never

find the body, and without a body, they can't prove it was me. And without proof, they wouldn't dare make a move.

But the witnesses. They could be a problem.

They won't be.

I've waded through deeper shit than this and come out clean, and I expect this won't be any different.

I push open the door of the booth and check the time on my phone. The gala should already be under way, and there's not a chance in hell I'm letting Keira miss the awards.

She doesn't know it, but I made certain that Seven Sinners was entered in multiple categories on a last-minute basis. I have zero control over the judging, but her product speaks for itself.

I also didn't tell her because if she doesn't win, there's the added bonus of not knowing she was in the running to begin with.

I'm not sure at what point I decided I needed to protect her from more than just physical threats, but also from what I know would be a crushing disappointment. This week has changed a lot of things.

I reach the suite and close the door behind me, listening for sounds of the stylists, but all is quiet. "Keira?"

"One second!" she calls from the vicinity of the bedroom. "I'm almost ready." She sounds much better than she did when I left.

I wait in the living room area and contemplate pouring myself another drink as my mind goes over J's call again, but decide against it.

Instead, I stare out the window I fucked Keira

against days ago. One more thing I wish I could repeat.

Fuck, I wish I could have this whole week again. But tonight, we go back to reality. The jet will be waiting on the tarmac for us as soon as the gala is finished.

"So, what do you think?"

I turn toward her voice as she steps into the bedroom doorway, and freeze.

Her dress, a brilliant green that matches her eyes, hugs every curve and yet conceals enough to be the epitome of class. Her hair is in some elaborate style with strands falling around her face.

"Jesus Christ."

"Is that a good *Jesus Christ* or a bad one?" she asks, stepping into the living room. The slit up one side of the dress flashes a toned leg and fuck-me shoes.

"That's a 'Jesus Christ, I hope you're not still hungover, because I don't know if I want to let you leave this room tonight.'"

Her lips curve into a smile. "Actually, I feel fine now. Must be the Irish in me." She gives me a once-over, her gaze stopping on my crotch. "You always look good in a suit, but you seem to have a minor problem."

"Don't ever refer to my dick as *minor*."

She laughs, and the sound reminds me of how freely she let it loose last night.

Fuck. I have to stop thinking about it.

She crosses the room, flashing a glimpse of leg with every step, a mischievous glint in her eyes.

THIRTY-SEVEN

Keira

BITS AND PIECES OF MY MEMORY RETURNED AS Brigid and Briana did my hair, makeup, and nails. They chattered away in the most adorable accents ever, asking what I've seen and done in Dublin. I had to fight to recall even those bits and pieces.

"I'm pretty sure we danced in a pub?" It came out as a question because even though the hazy recollection was there, it was hard to picture Mount, who I apparently called *Lachlan*, doing such a thing.

"Sounds like the *craic* was mighty," one of them said. I'd gotten their names mixed up as soon as they walked in the door.

"Crack? I don't do that. Crack is whack."

Both the girls laughed at me. "Not crack. The *craic*. The fun. A good time. You need to work on your Irish. You're definitely American, even though you blend in here lookin' like you do."

As they continued teaching me Irishisms, my mind

went elsewhere. Back to last night where I felt like I was trying to fit together a thousand-piece puzzle with no box to guide me.

Now, as I walk toward Lachlan in our suite, something has shifted. I feel that in my bones, and it terrifies me.

Then I remember what I said.

"Dance with me, Lachlan. Dance with me in Dublin."

And he did. I remember the feel of his body pressed against mine as we swayed to the slow songs, and the grip of his hands around my waist when he lifted me into the air like I weighed nothing.

The man I've thought was a monster has given me the best week of my life, and from what I recall, the best *night* of my life, and I have absolutely no idea how to handle that information.

This was only ever supposed to be sex. Repayment on a debt owed. But it has spiraled out of control, and now I'm terrified it's becoming something else entirely—which is impossible.

I know I have to shift the focus back to where it started. Sex. I need to wipe away my incomplete memories of last night because they're too good to be true.

The man who danced with me in a bar in a city I've wanted to see my entire life can never give me the happily-ever-after I thought I was getting once before. And not because he's a con like Brett was, but because he's *Lachlan Mount.*

I need to remind myself that I'm nothing but a possession to him, and we can never be anything more.

I stop a foot away from Lachlan. No, *Mount*, I

remind myself. I reach out with a new boldness and grab a handful of cock.

He sucks in the barest of breaths, no doubt shocked by my action.

See? I can do this. Whatever happened last night will be forgotten, and we'll be right back where we belong.

"No, it's definitely not minor." I lick my lips, devoid of lipstick because I told Brigid and Briana that I'd take care of that myself in case we were going to eat first.

"That's not exactly helping the problem either." His voice is rough and deep, like it takes everything he has to keep himself in check.

"You want to go downstairs like this?" I lift my gaze to his for a beat before dropping it again. His gaze is too intense for me. "If you walk into the ballroom like this, I can guarantee none of those wives will be able to look away."

He tilts my chin up, careful in his movements but still forcing my attention to his face. "Would that bother you?"

A blast of possessiveness blows through me as though I stepped in front of a raging fire. "Maybe," I say with a shrug.

"Then by all means, take care of it."

His words are a dare, one he thinks I won't take. But after last night, I don't have a clue what I want anymore, except to destroy any of the fairy tales I let myself believe, even if they were only for a moment.

I sweep my dress to the side and lower myself to my knees before him, then shoot a pointed look up at him. "Don't you dare mess up my hair."

His palms flex as though dying to do it anyway, but he forces them to grip the edge of the bar behind him.

I work his button and zipper free and finally wrap my hand around the hot thickness of his cock. This time, I feel powerful.

"What about your makeup?" he asks, his tone strangled.

"As long as you don't come on my face, we'll be fine."

When he doesn't answer, I lower my lips close enough to dart out my tongue and lick a bead of pre-cum from the head.

He groans, and I pull back.

"Deal?"

"Yes. Sweet fucking Christ, woman. Are you trying to make me beg?"

"It would be a nice change."

He growls down at me. "Go ahead and try."

THIRTY-EIGHT

Keira

"**F**UCK."

The satisfaction I get when he throws his head back and curses as I cup his balls in one hand and take his shaft deeper is probably unhealthy, but I don't care. As soon as he tossed down the challenge, I was on a mission.

The power struggle I understand is back, except this time, I have the advantage.

I drop my head to suck one ball into my mouth and then the other, and his groan fills the suite. I keep waiting for him to break my rule and destroy my hairstyle, which would give us both a reason not to leave the room, but he doesn't.

He's respecting my request, and that adds another layer to the power trip I'm already on.

I work his shaft, alternating my hand and mouth but never letting go of his balls, and glance up from beneath my eyelashes. His dark gaze spears me, and the raw need and desire in it has me ready to throw my advantage out the window. Hearing him beg pales in comparison to the thought of him yanking me to my feet, spinning me around, and burying his cock inside me.

What that says about me, I don't know or care at this moment.

"Are you going to swallow it all when I come down your throat?" he asks, and I shake my head. His brow furrows with confusion, and I let the head of his cock slide from my mouth with a pop. "What the hell game are you playing here?"

Slowly, I rise to my feet. "No game. Not this time."

Mount's eyes go molten. "You want to be fucked, don't you?"

I nod.

"Thank God."

He doesn't follow the story line I plotted out in my head, but when has he ever? Instead, he drags me toward the sofa, then pulls my dress up and out of the way as he bends me over the back. His breath catches when he sees I'm not wearing any panties.

"Naughty fucking girl. When we walk into that gala tonight, you're still going to feel me pounding inside you. Is that what you want?"

"Yes," I whisper.

"Louder."

"Yes, goddammit!"

"Then you better hold on, because I'm done holding back."

Mount is one hundred percent true to his word. An hour later, after I've repaired my makeup and fixed a few falling tendrils, I can still feel him as the ache pulses between my legs.

I'm still unsteady as we enter the gala. Hell, I'm still unsteady after my first drink. It's the Mount Effect, I decide.

Everyone's attention turns to the stage twenty minutes later when the emcee starts announcing winners of the competition. As I smile and clap, I wish more than ever I'd known I was coming because Seven Sinners is just as good, if not better, than those taking home awards tonight.

I open my mouth to tell Mount I need another drink, but the emcee hits the Tasters' Choice category for American whiskey, and I pause because this is the one I know we could have won.

"And the award goes to . . ." He opens the envelope dramatically before continuing. "Seven Sinners Distillery, the Spirit of New Orleans."

I look from side to side, wondering if anyone else heard what he said or if I'm still passed out drunk and hallucinating. *How is this possible?*

Mount's hand shifts from the small of my back, slipping around to pull me against his side. I look up at him, shock and confusion ripping through me.

"Did you do this? Set us up to win?"

He shakes his head. "All I did is make sure they took it as a late entry. Seven Sinners won this all on its own."

"Oh my God." Elation, brilliant and dazzling, fills me.

He jerks his chin toward the stage. "I believe it's time to accept your award."

With his hand on my back, we make our way through the crowd, but I climb the stairs to the podium by myself. My hands tremble as I accept the crystal-bottle statue and shake the emcee's hand.

"Thank you, sir." From my position on the stage, I scan the crowd, looking for only one face. And it's not one of my competitors.

It's *his*.

When I find it, another wave of exhilaration washes over me. He's smiling, and it's one I feel like I've only ever before seen in my garbled recollections of last night.

It's just as brilliant as I thought it would be.

The emcee gives me a nod. "It's our pleasure, Ms. Kilgore."

I swallow the emotions threatening to burst free of my chest and make my way back down the stairs. Mount is waiting at the bottom with a surprising expression on his face.

Pride.

"Congratulations, Madam President."

THIRTY-NINE

Mount

A S MUCH AS I WANT TO SPEND THE ENTIRE TRIP home initiating Keira into the mile-high club, I have to deal with business, and she busies herself doing the same. We work in silence for most of the flight, breaking our respective concentration to eat only once.

In my organization, I expect everyone to work hard, but even then, I rarely see someone with the same work ethic as I have.

But in front of me right now, and all this week, I've seen it in Keira.

I was a fool thinking I could take her, fuck her, and keep her in a little box on a shelf like any other toy.

But what the hell am I going to do with her now? Last night was an anomaly. When we get back to New Orleans, things have to return to the way they were. There are no other options.

Are you fucking kidding me? the voice in my head

challenges. *You're Lachlan Mount. You have the gold. You make the rules. That means you can have whatever the fuck you want.*

And what I want, more than anything, is to hear Keira call me by my first name again.

But this time . . . *sober.*

FORTY

Keira

'M NOT LOOKING AT HIM.

I'm not looking at him.

I. Am. Not. Looking. At. Him.

I fail and glance up for the hundredth time on this interminable flight, and take in the man before me.

I've used the word *never* so many times when it comes to Mount, only to break my vows, that I don't know what to think anymore.

Why does he have to be who he is? That's the conflict I can't get past. Somehow on this trip, I've convinced myself that if he were anyone else, everything would be different, and I would finally have found the one man who can give me everything I want and need. A partner.

But with each hour we spend in this plane, I can feel darkness gather around him like a tangible cloud, snuffing out the easiness of his posture that loosened more each day we were in Dublin.

I want a do-over.

I want a chance to revel in the differences that I didn't appreciate enough while we were there.

But I can't have that either.

When the wheels of the jet touch down on the runway at Lakefront Airport, I will go back to being Keira Kilgore, in debt to Lachlan Mount up to my eyeballs, my body his to use as he wishes in repayment.

Nothing will have changed, but at the same time, it feels like *everything* has.

I bury myself in work, expanding on all the notes I made after the distillery tour. I compose an email to Deegan Sullivan, thanking him personally and giving him an open invitation to come to Seven Sinners anytime he happens to be in New Orleans.

Then I start working on a plan for how we can implement safety measures in the most economical way so we can discuss starting tours of the distillery. For the first time, I don't give a single thought to what my father will say when he hears about it.

The crystal-bottle award lying beside me tells me that what we're doing at our little distillery matters, and it's my job to take us to the next level in any way I possibly can.

I tell myself I won't touch the capital in the bank unless I absolutely have to, because I want to be able to repay the debt.

But if I do that, what ties me to the man seated across from me? Nothing.

Only a week ago, I would have celebrated the idea.

There's something wrong with me. I can't possibly

feel this way.

By the time the tires hit the runway and the jet comes to a halt in front of the hangar, I've come to terms with something that terrifies me more than anything else ever has.

I don't hate Lachlan Mount.

Mount leads the way down the stairs, holding out a hand at the bottom. Before we left, I changed out of my gown and into a simple white blouse and a pair of dark skinny jeans. Mount didn't bother to change out of his suit. At this point, I consider it his natural uniform.

I expect to see Scar waiting for us with the usual car, but Mount strides toward the hangar door.

"Is he late? He's never late."

"V's not coming. I'm driving."

We step inside the large metal building, and a black muscle car with white racing stripes is parked inside.

"Whoa. Where did that come from?"

Mount glances over his shoulder as he walks to the wall to punch a code into a keypad next to a metal box. "My collection."

When the door swings open, he pulls out the keys and closes it again. He uses one to open the trunk, and I take a step back.

"What? Afraid there's going to be a body inside?"

"Is that humor? Did you just make a joke?"

An airport employee comes rushing in with our luggage before Mount can respond. Once the luggage is in the trunk, he unlocks the passenger side door for me.

"I don't joke."

"Bullshit," I say, unable to stop myself.

His eyes narrow on me. "The rules are different now—"

"Now that we're back? I'm getting that." I settle myself in the seat and huff out a harsh laugh. "I wouldn't expect anything else from you. After all, you have your reputation to uphold, and you never know who's watching here."

As his expression darkens, I look away, focusing on the award cradled in my lap. One piece of tangible proof I actually get to keep from this trip.

Mount slams my door and rounds the hood. When he takes the driver's side of the bench seat and jams the keys into the ignition, I know I've hit the nail on the head.

Even if he wanted to be the man he was in Ireland, it's not possible here.

The engine roars to life, its growl perfectly suiting the temperament of the man driving it. He lets it warm up for a few minutes, both of us sitting in tense silence, before he backs it out and guns it.

I stare out the window, but instead of soaking up every bit of the city like I did in Dublin, I see nothing as we fly through the familiar streets.

I'm one hundred percent certain he's breaking speed limits, but what cop would give him a ticket for it? He probably has most of them on his payroll.

We close in on the French Quarter, and instead of

taking one of the convoluted routes I'm used to Scar driving, Mount heads through the heart of it toward home.

Home.

I scoff at the word silently. That's not what it is, and I'm an idiot if I think it's anything but the same lavish prison cell it was before we left.

We're not dancing in Dublin anymore.

Mount slows for a few pedestrians at a stop sign before punching the gas and jerking the wheel hard to the right. The car rockets forward, tires squealing, and his body swings toward me as he turns.

"Fuck!"

What the hell?

His body arches further toward mine, and everything turns to chaos.

People say when traumatic things happen, the world decelerates so you can see it unfold in slow motion.

It doesn't work like that for me.

The driver's side window shatters, glass shards flying everywhere. The only thing I comprehend is *pain* as Mount jerks the wheel again and my head slams against my window. The car crashes into a lamppost before toppling it and coming to a halt.

Pop. Pop. Pop.

Holes punch through the spiderwebbed windshield.

Shocked, I struggle to draw in a breath, but I can't.

"Keira!"

Mount's yell sounds faint as the world fades

around me.

I blink twice, my lids heavier each time. My head sags forward and I blink again.

When did my shirt turn red?

"Look at me! Keira!"

I try to lift my head, but it's heavy.

He struggles with the seat belt, ripping it off before he leans toward me. More red drips off his hand as he reaches for my face.

Is that . . . blood? My thoughts go fuzzier.

"Stay with me, Keira. Please. Fucking. Stay. With. Me."

I hear his orders, but they grow fainter with each word. My eyes slip closed.

"No!" It's like a lion whispering in the jungle.

Someone lifts my head, and I force my lids open once more, just for a second. It's long enough to see the pain, fury, and devastation in his dark gaze.

"Lachlan?"

"Stay with me. I'm not going to fucking lose you now!"

"Can't. Breathe." My eyes slide shut again as sirens wail in the distance, and Lachlan Mount yells my name before everything goes completely silent.

Lachlan and Keira's story will conclude in

SINFUL
EMPIRE

ALSO BY MEGHAN MARCH

Take Me Back

Bad Judgment

BENEATH SERIES:
Beneath These Shadows
Beneath This Mask
Beneath This Ink
Beneath These Chains
Beneath These Scars
Beneath These Lies
Beneath the Truth

DIRTY BILLIONAIRE TRILOGY:
Dirty Billionaire
Dirty Pleasures
Dirty Together

DIRTY GIRL DUET:
Dirty Girl
Dirty Love

REAL DUET:
Real Good Man
Real Good Love

REAL DIRTY DUET:
Real Dirty
Real Sexy

FLASH BANG SERIES:
Flash Bang
Hard Charger

AUTHOR'S NOTE

UNAPOLOGETICALLY SEXY ROMANCE

I'd love to hear from you. Connect with me at:

Website: www.meghanmarch.com
Facebook: www.facebook.com/MeghanMarch-
Author
Twitter: www.twitter.com/meghan_march
Instagram: www.instagram.com/meghanmarch

ABOUT THE AUTHOR

Meghan March has been known to wear camo face paint and tromp around in the woods wearing mud-covered boots, all while sporting a perfect manicure. She's also impulsive, easily entertained, and absolutely unapologetic about the fact that she loves to read and write smut.

Her past lives include slinging auto parts, selling lingerie, making custom jewelry, and practicing corporate law. Writing books about dirty-talking alpha males and the strong, sassy women who bring them to their knees is by far the most fabulous job she's ever had.

She loves hearing from her readers at meghanmarchbooks@gmail.com.

90074050R00152

Made in the USA
Columbia, SC
26 February 2018